"Don't y[ou] [lecture] me, Jude Radcliffe!"

Corey went on furiously. "You're pretty impetuous and irresponsible yourself—kissing girls you think are engaged and trying to seduce girls in woods and bursting into people's houses while they're having a bath—"

"Oh, grow up, Corey!" he thundered. "We've set off something between us that's taking over. I don't like what's happening, either, but don't deny it. It's something special."

"Then you weren't trying to seduce me?" she asked.

"Of course I was trying to seduce you," he began.

"Mr. Radcliffe, I said I'd sort out your lodge gardens, and I will. But that's the extent of our relationship. I can't bear to be tucked into someone else's pocket or to be out of my class. So go and take a cold bath, and I promise not to look in your window while you're having it!"

SARA WOOD lives in a rambling sixteenth-century home in the medieval town of Lewes amid the Sussex hills. Her sons have claimed the cellar for bikes, making ferret cages, taxidermy and winemaking, while Sara has virtually taken over the study with her reference books, word processor and what have you. Her amiable, tolerant husband, she says, squeezes in wherever he finds room. After having tried many careers—secretary, guest house proprietor, play-group owner and primary teacher—she now finds writing romance novels gives her enormous pleasure.

Books by Sara Wood

HARLEQUIN ROMANCE
2814—PERFUMES OF ARABIA

SARA WOOD

passion's daughter

Harlequin Books

TORONTO • NEW YORK • LONDON
AMSTERDAM • PARIS • SYDNEY • HAMBURG
STOCKHOLM • ATHENS • TOKYO • MILAN

Harlequin Presents first edition May 1987
ISBN 0-373-10981-4

Original hardcover edition published in 1986
by Mills & Boon Limited

CHAPTER ONE

JUDE RADCLIFFE strolled to the tall Georgian windows, bored with his own company, unsettled as yet in his new home. After Florida, the warm English summer seemed cool and he reached for a light jacket to shrug on over his thin shirt.

He had dismissed the idea of going to bed. Despite two nights in his London flat and nearly a week here, his internal clock was still re-adjusting and he was wide awake, even at two in the morning. In any case, he would have been unable to sleep for the sublime silence. The unusual stillness contrasted so dramatically with the unending dash-and-crash of the last two years that it gave him a feeling that his life was pausing at long last, providing a breathing space for reassessing objectives.

'And now for a short intermission,' he murmured to himself.

Yet it was odd, this sensation that surrounded him. It was not a restful peace but a hanging-fire, a waiting. In his bones he knew it had something to do with Corey.

Thinking of her stirred him into action. Raising his arms, he slid up the sash window, breathing in the fragrance of the golden rose which clambered up the grey stone walls. Down below his bedroom window, past the terrace, swept the vast lawns of Sedgewood Manor. So far, only a small area of grass had been shorn by the mower; the rest grew in wild disarray,

merging with shrubs and borders in one scrambling
jungle.

A pure and startlingly loud warble trilled through
the calm, its piercing quality sending a small shiver
down Jude's back. The sound drew his eyes to the
meadow past the lawns and towards the dark woods
beyond. What he saw made him grip the sill and lean
far out, wondering for a moment if the silvered light
from the moon had created an optical illusion. A
slender figure was flitting through the widely spaced
trees on the fringe of the wood, a figure distinguish-
able only by the flimsy, drifting white dress.

It had to be Corey. Discounting ghosts, who else
would inhabit Sedge Wood in the early hours of the
morning? All day long he'd had a nagging, unfinished
feeling as though he was on the brink of something
momentous. Was it just his tired, jet-lagged, overworked mind, or had she bewitched him?

Meeting her, in all her impulsiveness and elusive-
ness, had set his mind into overdrive. With her vivid
attack on life, she had evoked the memory of his youth
in its recklessness and defiance of convention. Corey
had made him realise just how far his own image had
changed. In the business world he was still considered
something of an eccentric; in her eyes he was stuffy.
Jude's eyes flashed angrily. It was an image he had
never expected to acquire, yet it had happened, and
escaped his notice until now.

His return to England had arisen from a dissatisfac-
tion with the way his life was going. More and more
frequently came the urge to kick over the traces. He
envied Corey.

The country scene, filled now with the soaring
clarity of the extraordinary bird-song, mocked his
teeming thoughts of the free sprite who had captivated

him. Adrenalin raced through his body as he felt a compelling urge to make an unscheduled and ill-considered rendezvous with her, there in the wood. It would be the action of a fool.

A fool who'd been knocked for six by an impact almost as sudden as the impact she'd made on his favourite mare!

As far as Corey was concerned, that summer evening a few days ago had started normally enough. For a start, she was late. Time figured little in her life—that was one of the advantages of being self-employed.

By the neat grandmother clock against the chimney-breast, it was seven o'clock already and here she was, still standing up in the tin bath, soaping her slim body dreamily, smoothing long, artistic hands almost sensuously over her olive-sheen skin and singing softly to herself.

Reluctantly she bent for the enamel jug beside the bath and sluiced away the suds, stepping on to the thick forest-green towel laid on her sitting room floor.

'Well,' she announced to the sleek black cat stretching its feline length across her chintz armchair, 'Tom's gang might not like what they see, but it'll be clean!'

She scowled. What a boring evening ahead! The dreaded family dinner. Corey tucked the towel around her sinuous body and slowly padded up the steep stairs to the bedroom. Really she ought to hurry. An internal devil was encouraging her to put off the evil hour when she'd meet Tom's crowd. Living always for the present, heedless for the future, it hadn't occurred to her to worry about the occasion until Tom began to give her instructions on how to behave at the dinner. He'd advised her on topics of conversation and then informed her that his boss was coming too!

Her small nose wrinkled in distaste. In the two years that she had known Tom, he had repeatedly bored her socks off with anecdotes about Mr 'Tycoon' Radcliffe. Even though the wretched man had been building up a subsidiary company somewhere in America all that time, he still exerted quite an influence over his staff with his frequent memos and telephone calls: short, abrupt, pertinent and occasionally ruthless, according to Tom. Now he'd apparently returned and he and Tom would no doubt spend the whole evening discussing business while the women gossipped about clothes and holidays. Ugh!

Grumbling, she scrambled into a pair of thin briefs and slid into the dress which hung, dazzling white, against the pine door. Full-length broderie anglaise dresses were way out of date, and the vivid orange sash flamed its defiance of decorum, clashing violently with the brilliant reds and yellows of her bedroom. She sucked in her breath and smoothed the tight bodice into place, unravelling the trailing sash and tying it firmly around her slender waist. Wow, it was bright!

Her sudden grin flashed gleaming white teeth at the mirror and set her coffee-brown eyes dancing with delight. Carefully she adjusted the low neckline of the dress to sit seductively off the shoulders. They would probably have a fit when they saw the amount of flesh she was exposing. But she was on show tonight. Selected friends and Tycoon Radcliffe were gathering to see the kind of girl that good old Tom was marrying. They'd sure see a lot of her top half!

She scrutinised the striking, rather overstated effect critically. This creature in the mirror, twenty-two, financially independent and about to marry a pukka

Gowrie-Dyson, had come a long way from the battered old van that had been her first home. An impish smile touched her face. Now she was in a battered old cottage! And though some people in the village disapproved of her Bohemian life-style, no one humiliated her any more. Her relationship with Tom had seen to that. Very respectable. Whenever she had doubts about settling down with Tom, she resurrected the misery of her first day at school in far-off Birmingham.

'Eleven years old and you can't read!' the teacher had cried, setting all the class into uproar.

'I bin busy!' she'd yelled angrily. That initial response established the basis for years of torment.

Only now was she losing her inferiority complex, with Tom's help. He was quite a dear, really—a bit serious, maybe, but then weren't most young men eager for promotion? Even so, a small, nagging doubt entered her mind. It was squashed resolutely, as always.

Her hair looked too tidy, now she had brushed it. Bending forwards, she hung her head upside down till her thick hair hung freely in heavy coils, as blue-black and feathered as a raven's wing. Then she straightened, flinging it into a satisfyingly wild disarray.

On impulse, she rummaged amongst her undies until she found a cluster of wild silk poppies and fixed them around a black comb in her hair. The image in the mirror looked back at her and she winced. Maybe she ought to get some Suitable Clothes. She always seemed to look like a gipsy.

'Damn you!' she raged at her reflection. 'Why aren't you more comfortable in nice polyester suits and neat haircuts?'

Corey ground her teeth belligerently. And damn her

olive skin, too. Tom's family must be blind not to put
two and two together. If they found out about her
background, they'd put off the wedding like a shot. It
was almost tempting, to test Tom's love. But she didn't
trust him that far. He was too conventional and she
liked him too much to risk losing him. There came
that doubt again. Out, damned doubt!

Gathering up a soft, flame-coloured shoulder bag,
she hurtled out of the lodge door, slamming it violently
behind her. By the time she had manoeuvred her
white Mini into the narrow country lane, she had
nearly chewed all the coral lipstick from her high-
arched mouth.

'Stop rushing so fast,' she muttered at the clock in
the car. Tom hated her to be late. She had better do an
about-turn and take the short cut past her lodge house
and through the manor land. No one lived there now
that old Mr Wallace was dead.

Careering up the drive, she scorched past the grand
oval lawn, now dreadfully overgrown, and screamed
around the stable block corner on two wheels.

Too late, she noticed a blur of movement in front of
her: a terrifying flash of white muscle and rolling eyes.
Then, to the sound of a sickening thud, she had
jammed on the brakes. The seat-belt crushed the
breath out of her as it checked the forward motion,
snapping her head back to hit the restraint. Her door
was wrenched open. A stream of abuse in a rich
country brogue assailed her ears. Someone was trying
to drag her out of the car: a short and wiry someone
with a cloth cap topping his furious, distorted face.

'Silas! Shut up and come over here!' bellowed a
deeper voice.

Silas seemed to be the Angry Cloth Cap man, since
he disappeared immediately from her view. She closed

her eyes, trying to calm her nerves. Almost at once she opened them wide again. A horse was whinnying, a pained wheeze of a sound. Hand on her churning stomach, Corey looked straight ahead and saw the large body of a white mare lying across the brick roadway. Her eyes clouded in distress.

Oh dear heaven, let it be alive! This was just the sort of result her impulsive, thoughtless actions led her to. This was why she was marrying Tom: to gain some control over her headlong, eventful life.

Another crumpled breath from the horse galvanised her into action. She fumbled for the clasp of her seatbelt and staggered out shakily, all thoughts with the wounded animal, wondering how long those white flanks would continue to heave, how long before one of the men raised a gun and . . .

Silas spun around as her Mini's door clunked shut.

'Keep away from 'er! You get away. You done enough damage for one day,' he growled.

'No, please, I can . . .'

'Do as you're told,' rapped a harsh voice.

The other man crouched behind the horse, his broad, high forehead shining strangely dark in the rays of the setting sun. For a brief moment his leadgrey eyes flashed icy hate at her, then he continued to run his hands expertly over the mare.

'But I . . .'

'Stay back, shut up and keep out of our way till we're ready for you,' he ordered.

His accent alone would have crushed Corey. It announced a life of privilege, public schools and exclusive clubs. It was unaffected, yet with every word carefully enunciated. What with meeting him, and with Tom's guests to come, her inferiority complex was getting a bashing tonight!

Effectively silenced for the moment, she stood
sullenly twisting her trailing sash, while the man spoke
urgently to the groom.

'Silas, telephone the vet. Immediately.'

'Right, Mr Radcliffe.'

A wave of horror swept through Corey. Could it be
Tom's boss? He was the right age—about thirty-five
or six. That dark skin might just be the tan he'd
acquired in Florida, not a trick of the light, and he
certainly had an 'independent tycoon' air of authority.
The accent fitted, the athletic frame fitted—and the
sharp, peremptory orders fitted Tom's description too.

With a pang of dismay, Corey saw that he was
wearing a finely tailored dinner-jacket, flung wide to
show a neatly pleated shirt which clung tightly to the
tapering curves of his body. How many Radcliffes in
the area were about to go out for dinner? Hell fire,
what a way to meet the man she was supposed to
impress for Tom!

Miserably, she tucked her disordered hair behind
her ears in an automatic gesture, setting the silver
bangles on her arm jangling. The movement made
him look up and his hard eyes swept critically over
her, for all the world as if he were assessing her market
value and finding it negligible.

For a moment, his gaze rested speculatively on her
fingers, frowning to see a silver ring on each one, then
he compressed his lips and returned to his gentle
examination. He must have touched a tender place,
for the mare tossed her head, flecking Radcliffe with
light foam. Corey's soft heart overcame her insecurity
and embarrassment.

'Let me help, I know something about horses,' she
pleaded in her husky, honey voice.

Radcliffe glanced up briefly.

'You touch her over my dead body,' he snarled. 'God damn you, woman!'

Handling the mare, he had been partially restrained, but no longer. He stood and faced her, his anger escaping like a torrent.

'You stupid female! Did you think you were a marauding army, invading my land? What in God's name were you doing to come like a bat out of hell down my drive? This is private property! And *this*,' his finger quivered with the force of his rage, 'this is a bloody expensive horse. If you've injured her badly, you'll be the one to shoot her. I warn you, if she is . . .' Words seemed to fail him at last. The slanting brows forked menacingly, his mouth twisted.

'I'm sorry. I *know* that's inadequate, but what else can I say? It was my fault.'

'You're damn right it was. And I'll see you pay for it, believe me!'

Corey blanched at the threat. Oh Lord, Tom was sure to hear of this. He'd be so cross. Tom! They'd all be waiting for her. She would be even later now. Still, they'd be waiting for Radcliffe, too. In for a penny, in for a pound, she had to know the results of her hectic driving. She knelt on the ground, oblivious that the dark earth, damp from a summer storm, was muddying the white dress.

'Get up,' grated the man, his grey eyes graphite-hard.

'Hell fire!' flashed Corey, glad that the mare was between them. 'I've got to know the damage.'

Her hands slid gently over the sweating body. Soon, without knowing that she did so, she was murmuring softly to the trembling mare, crooning phrases she had forgotten since her childhood. She'd learnt the words at the horse fairs when the men prepared an unruly pony for sale. Gradually the mare relaxed, her breath becoming less harsh.

In relief, Corey sat back on her heels.

'I'm pretty sure she's just badly winded—and maybe bruised. No serious damage.' She looked up at the taut, slim man. He ran long slender fingers through the brown waves that tumbled on to his high forehead.

'Well, aren't you the lucky one,' he said with venom.

'The vet's coming right 'way,' said Silas, striding up to Radcliffe.

'Right. Stay with Moonlight. I must make a phone call. I'll be late for that damn dinner. Take this woman's name and address while I'm gone.' He glared at the muddied girl with the worried brown eyes. 'Let me tell you, Miss Helter Skelter, that you'll be hearing from my solicitor. I only hope you weren't planning on any holidays for a few years: I intend to sue for damages. Of all the mindless, heedless, irresponsible women drivers . . . there ought to be a special test for women like you!'

Abruptly, the outward signs of fury receded and he assumed a mask of composure, remote and stiff. Just like Tom's crowd. Sleek, impersonal, another executive clone. Only those slanting brows and the fullness of his lips set him a little apart, otherwise he was the epitome of the formal, right-wing businessman. She was being stifled by them. It was like buses, she thought inconsequentially: once you came across one, you were inundated with dozens more.

'Get into that deadly weapon of yours,' he continued, 'and see if you can drive off my land without killing anyone or anything. And if you happen to live round here, make sure you never come near the Manor again!'

His even tone belied the furious words. He made her feel like a stupid schoolgirl again. Wait till he met her again at the dinner party! Should she introduce herself now, or face him later? Better to leave him to stew for a while: when he knew there was nothing wrong with the horse he'd probably calm down.

She sighed. The evening was going to be even more horrific than she had originally feared.

'There's no need to be sour, your horse is all right,' she said defiantly. 'I've said I'm sorry and I am, really. But no one's been here for months, you see . . .'

'Save your life story. I don't want to know. Get out!'

Eyes blazing, Corey drew herself to her full height to confront him on more equal terms. 'You're so concerned with your horse. I suppose it never occurred to you that I might have hurt myself!' she yelled shrewishly, then swung sharply around, teetering a little on the white sandals. She was wearing shoes as a concession to Tom and found the sensation unbalancing. Before he could say anything more, she ran to the Mini and started it up, reversing till she had room to turn, watching the tensed figure standing protectively by the stricken horse.

Twenty minutes later she was knocking on the door of the elegant town house where Tom's parents, the Gowrie-Dysons, lived. The door was opened by her fiancé who stood frowning irritably at her.

'Oh, Tom, please,' she begged, 'don't start on me. I've had enough of angry men for one day.'

'Oh, really. Some time we'll discuss what you've been up to and whose toes you've trodden on,' seethed Tom, 'but for now, dinner's nearly ruined and

Mother's even more furious than I am. How can you be so rude?'

'I had an accident,' began Corey.

Tom eyed the filthy hem of her skirt and the mud splatters spoiling the dazzling white. 'So I see. You certainly look a mess. It's moments like this that I wonder ... Well, you'll have to go in and apologise and be as nice as pie to make up.'

He turned away and she stared in amazement. These men! One cared more about his horse—well, that was understandable really—but Tom cared more about a rotten dinner! For all he knew, she could have been shocked, or even injured. Setting her mouth grimly, she strode into the drawing room.

'Corey dear!' cried Tom's mother sweetly, masking a brief look of horror at Corey's appearance. 'So sorry you were delayed. Isn't she charming, everyone? This is Corey ... Tom's fiancée. Quite the little Bohemian. An artist, you know. This is Daphne and John Steadman, Christabel and Philip Grey, and Lydia Farley.'

Corey shook hands with everyone, noticing with grim delight their hesitation in taking her grubby hand.

'I'm sure you'd like to pop into the cloakroom for a moment,' observed Tom's mother.

Corey agreed. She'd better wash off the honest horse sweat before she ate. Obediently she made her way out of the drawing room, only to hear Mrs Gowrie-Dyson's clarion call ringing after her.

'So hard for the poor girl, living in quite absolutely primitive conditions. Tom can't wait to get her into civilisation.'

Damn civilisation, cursed Corey, trying to decide which soap had the least cloying perfume. She mussed up her hair again and tried to clean up her hands and feet; the stains on the dress were best left alone. They'd all seen them already and so had Radcliffe. Bet he didn't get the same angry welcome from Tom because *he* was late.

When she returned, Tom's mother was still warbling on about her.

'. . . but we forgive her. She brings such vivacity and originality to our dull old lives.'

They all laughed politely, but Corey could tell what they all thought. *That* little ragamuffin, marrying Tom? Wouldn't help him much, in his ponderous march towards a directorship! As they laughed, Corey shrank a little, disconcerted by the sheer expensive elegance of the four chic women in their pastel chiffon cocktail dresses. Chiffon was obviously 'in' this season. In her startling colouring and the zinging orange sash and lipstick, she felt very garish and over-dramatic—and over-exposed.

'Paranoia is setting in, girl,' thought Corey. 'No one gives a toss about you really, as long as you behave.'

Mr Gowrie-Dyson wandered over with her favourite drink and kissed her on both cheeks. 'Made it a bit stronger than usual. I can see you've been in a scrape. Now, are you . . .'

His wife interrupted. 'Darlings! Food! Come, I'm famished. We're not to wait for Jude, he phoned. Hurry along, or the staff will walk out on me and Lord knows how I'd cope.'

With an apologetic shrug, Tom's father patted her arm and handed her to Tom. 'Look after her, feller, she's had a tumble. Bit upset, you know.'

'Upset!' Tom slicked back his short blond hair and propelled her into the pseudo-Georgian dining room. 'I'm the one who should be upset. Shown up in front of

all my friends! Corey—what on *earth* is that smell?'
He bent his neat blond head closer.

'Now, now you two,' carolled his mother, 'what are
you saying to each other? Corey's gone quite puce!'

'Lettice darling,' came Lydia's husky voice, 'olive-
skinned girls don't go puce. The skin tone is too green
for that.'

Cow, thought Corey. Lydia was a cool, soignée
blonde, carefully groomed, subtly feminine. She
decided that she disliked Lydia slightly more than she
disliked Tom's mother. How she was hating this
evening! Whatever had possessed her to get mixed up
with these people? She was way out of her depth. They
made her feel uneasy and very gauche. Apart from
Tom's parents, she hadn't really met any of his friends
properly before—she'd avoided doing so in sheer self-
defence, pleading shyness. Most of them were
accountants as he was, not the more interesting
creative workers at Radcliffe Property Consortium.

'Tucking up next to me, eh?' queried Philip Grey, as
Lettice waved her to the centre chair.

'It looks like it,' agreed Corey without enthusiasm.
She was also right opposite the dreaded Lydia. Next to
Mrs Gowrie-Dyson was an empty chair, waiting,
presumably for Jude Radcliffe. If only he'd come and
get it all over.

An arm reached out and placed a crystal finger bowl
to her right. Corey stared at the slice of lemon floating
in it, wickedly considering drinking it, sucking the
lemon, or diluting her drink. Anything to liven up the
proceedings. She caught a glimpse of Tom's fresh,
eager face, looking at her pleadingly, pursed her lips at
him and grinned to see his relief when she unwrapped
her napkin instead. He must have read her thoughts—
was she so transparent, or totally predictable? Her

grin turned to dismay as the first course was presented. Artichokes! She was sure that Mrs Gowrie-Dyson had chosen them on purpose, guessing she would have no idea how to eat them.

'Do be the first to try them, Corey darling,' called Tom's mother from the other end of the table. 'And tell me if you think they're quite ready.'

Everyone watched, expectantly.

'Mr Radcliffe,' announced the maid.

Tom's boss couldn't have chosen a better time to arrive. In all the flurry that arose as he was greeted and soothed with a large straight whisky, Corey relaxed in relief, the only one still at the table, since everyone had surprisingly wandered over to him. Like bees round the honey pot, she thought. Well, he was the provider of a fat income for most of them, it was only natural they should be paying homage.

His deep voice was holding them enthralled as he related the recent events involving her.

'. . . As you can imagine, I just couldn't believe it. It was the act of a total maniac. I suppose all the locals have been using the Manor as a racing track lately. If I'd known, I would have strung chains across the drive. How my horse escaped so lightly, I don't know. Mrs Gowrie-Dyson, please don't let me hold up your dinner any more. I do apologise.'

'Nonsense! Quite understandable. What an awful experience for you. Corey, what are you doing over there? What a shy thing you are! Come along and shake hands with Jude Radcliffe.'

With great reluctance she rose, slowly placing her napkin on the table, her eyes lowered. Radcliffe caught his breath with a sharp zhut!

'You are Tom's fiancée?' he asked coldly.

'I am. How do you do.' Corey shook his hand firmly,

meeting his eyes with a challenge. 'Tom isn't responsible for the things I do, you must realise that,' she stated.

His mouth tightened. 'Just as well. One irrational member of his family is enough.'

She tossed her head, scowling. 'I'm not a member of his family yet.'

'No.' He considered her carefully, with remote eyes. 'Well, Tom, Corey isn't quite what I expected.'

'Er, no.' Tom flushed crimson. 'She's usually quite—quite——' He floundered miserably and Corey fumed, glaring at his lack of support.

'Taking up your parting words,' broke in Jude smoothly, '*were* you hurt? Was there any damage apart from your dress and your hairstyle?'

'My hair always looks like this,' Corey ground out tightly. 'I hate primpy styles. This one's free-ranging, like my hens.'

Jude's eyebrows slanted upwards in surprise.

'What *is* going on?' asked Lydia petulantly.

Corey faced the fascinated guests. 'It was me who crashed into Mr Radcliffe's horse. Or it was I. Whatever is right. I was haring through his stables and went slap bang into this Moonlight.'

There was a moment's silence as they digested the news.

'That explains the smell of horse sweat, or is it dung?' claimed Lydia in a stage whisper. Then more loudly, she announced, 'Two things one never does, darling: damage a man's car or damage his horse. I'm surprised Jude is even speaking to you.'

'Jude won't be speaking to anyone if he dies of starvation,' he murmured.

Whether it was his intention or not, Corey was grateful to him for diverting attention to himself.

'Let's forget the incident. I think I see some delicious looking starters on the table,' he continued briskly.

He was quickly seated next to Tom's mother and soon attacked the artichoke, peeling off the leaves deftly and dipping the fleshy bases in melted butter. He didn't bother with the finger bowl, delighting Corey by sucking the dripping golden butter from his fingers with relish. When she felt the trickle of butter dribbling down her chin, she slicked it up neatly with a whisk of her index finger, catching an amused and approving glance from Jude as she did so.

Lettice Gowrie-Dyson noticed too, but the action did not win her approval at all. She made a great show of dipping the tips of her fingers into the crystal bowl before dynamiting Corey with the question she always did her utmost to avoid encouraging.

'Corey,' she called, 'isn't it about time we met your mother—and your brother? Even if we're giving you the reception as a gift,' she paused to smile dismissively at her own generosity, 'there are family things to talk about.'

Playing for time, Corey reached for her wine glass and took a large gulp.

'It's so difficult to trace them,' she said vaguely. 'They move around too much. I've no idea where they are.'

'How interesting,' murmured Lydia. 'What do they do, then?'

Fortifying herself with wine once more, Corey eyed Lydia suspiciously.

'They're both artists,' she said curtly, and turned to Tom frantically, but curiosity was getting the better of him and he had heard Corey stalling about her family for too long.

'What kind of artists, darling?' he asked.

She sucked distractedly at a chunk of artichoke core and took another drink. 'Mother works with silk and Salf carves.' Her face was sullen. Why wouldn't they lay off?

'Corey and Salf. Very unusual,' said Jude quietly. 'You obviously have an imaginative mother.'

'His name is really Persalf,' offered Corey, wondering why on earth she had done so.

'Middle European, isn't it?' persisted Jude, then stopped suddenly. Huge melting-chocolate eyes were turned to him, broadcasting their distress. 'Talking of names,' he said loudly, to the seated guests, 'have I ever told you of the names my mother intended to inflict on me? Achilles Adonis. Can you credit it? I'd been conceived on a Greek beach after a particularly raucous night in a taverna—it's all right, Mrs Gowrie-Dyson, it was their honeymoon—and my mother thought she ought to thank the gods. Father said it would be more appropriate if I was called Retsina!'

He held the rapt, amused audience. Was it coincidence, or had he responded to her need?

'And why did they settle on Jude?' she asked breathlessly, trying to prolong the diversion.

'My father pointed out that if I was called Achilles then everyone would say I was a heel. And fortunately he knew more Greek history than Mother. He told her that Adonis might have been born beautiful, as I undoubtedly was,' he paused for the ripple of laughter around the table, 'but he was also born of incest. So she settled rather rapidly for Jude—which means "praise".'

They all began to exchange stories about their

names after that, then the conversation meandered in a desultory way, conversation that Corey was unable to join in, knowing nothing of their life-styles. She retreated further into herself. It was becoming more and more apparent that she didn't fit in Tom's world. She had been very stupid not to have faced facts before. It was typical of her that she hadn't thought things through properly—and she was typically in a mess as a result. What the hell was she going to do?

It didn't help that Jude Radcliffe's stone-grey eyes kept drifting in her direction, disturbing her with their odd, watching quality. It was as if he was adding her up and beginning to find answers. To escape eye-contact with him, she affected nonchalance by sipping her wine repeatedly. In the warmth of the summer evening, she grew flushed, reckless and silently obdurate.

Lydia seemed bent on dazzling Jude. She kept tilting her small, pointed face to his hard, carved one. How obvious can you get! thought Corey savagely. But they belonged to the same sphere, those two—terribly polite, smoothly coping with the world. Both looked sophisticated enough to deal with any unpleasant situation that arose. Corey had heard— interminably—how Jude Radcliffe had turned his father's interior design business into a vast empire that served the jet-set in Europe and America. You had to be pretty sharp and calculating to achieve all that in ten years.

She looked around the table at the smooth young men paying homage to the smoothest of them all, Jude Radcliffe. In a few months she might be giving a similar dinner party, entertaining guests like this. She'd certainly have to entertain *him*—and sit next to him as her principal guest, making witty conversation.

The prospect made her heart sink.

'Ladies?' Mrs Gowrie-Dyson raised her eyebrows. 'Shall we leave the men to their port?'

Obediently, the women followed her through the door, whisking subtle perfumes and a swish of chiffon in their wake.

'Corey,' muttered Tom, jerking his head in his mother's direction.

'No, thank you, I'll stay,' she said firmly refusing to comply with such an archaic tradition. She was damned if she'd withdraw to watch the women powder their faces and listen to their banal chatter. 'I like port.'

Tom's face paled. 'You can't! I mean . . .'

'Tom, this is the age of independent women,' drawled Jude in amusement. 'You should indulge your fiancée. Well, Corey, do you draw the line at cigars, or would you like one of mine?'

'The port will be enough,' she said, bridling at his patronising tone.

'More than enough,' said Tom tightly. 'In fact, if you'll excuse us, Corey and I have one or two things to discuss. We'll go outside for a moment.'

Jude's eyes swivelled to Corey's, clearly expecting— and hoping, she thought—to hear her disagree. She tossed back the hair which had swooped down to cover one eye and stood up, holding on to the table for support. Her legs felt very odd, quite mushy.

'Suits me fine,' she said. 'Don't worry, Mr Radcliffe, Tom won't be led astray by an eccentric wife. You can relax. Your tame executive won't be developing ulcers because of me.'

He sipped his port without dropping his cool grey eyes from her glowing brown ones, drawn irrevocably by the startling and dramatic quality that exuded from her. 'Good,' he said lazily, admiring the sway of her shoulders as she strolled out.

In the garden, Tom faced her, hands on his hips. She forestalled his attack, flinging her arms wide in a theatrical attitude of renunciation.

'It won't work, will it?' she said impetuously. 'I'm hopeless. I don't have the right background, I've no idea how to eat half the food your mother serves up. My curl—cultural background is too hazy for me to have a clue about any of these operas and clever plays that everyone raves about. I feel uncomfortable with your crowd.'

'Look, love——' began Tom.

'Shut up, Tom, I'm in full flow. Listen. I know I'm tizzy, but I'd never dare say this otherwise. You just don't know how much I'm chucking up by acknolly-ack . . . owning up to my inad . . . oh hell! The things I can't do! For years I've tried to prove I'm better than I am.'

'You're fantastic, it's just . . .'

'Yes, just that I'm raw around the edges and untrained and illogical.'

'You said you loved me,' said Tom quietly, seeing how serious she was.

'I know, I know. And I thought I did. You were the first person to respond positively to me. I liked the glow in your eyes. I like *you*. You're kind and I trust you. But to live with you forever . . . Tom, I'm discovering there's more to marriage than the two of you—that's only the start. I have to take on some of your life-style. You've got different standards from mine and I think you let all the wrong things worry you. There's no way I could live your sort of life. Here's your ring. It was all a mistake.'

'Hold on, hold on.' Tom refused the ring. 'You and

your outbursts! You must learn to think before you speak,' he scolded. 'It's your ring, anyway. You made it.'

'You paid for it,' she retorted.

'Blunt as ever! Corey, calm down. You were nervous tonight. Driving into Radcliffe's horse threw you off balance. You didn't do too badly tonight, considering.'

'Grateful thanks, O Prince. Oh, hell! You're making it worse! How can a man as young as you sound so pompous? Why do I get this trapped feeling when I'm with you? You like rituals, I hate them. Routine drives me mad. Do you know that you say "See you later" every time you say goodbye?'

'What's wrong with that?' he asked, puzzled.

'*Every* time, *every* evening?'

'I don't understand. Look, I think this is pre-wedding blues. You'll be O.K. when you settle down.'

'*No*, I won't! I don't want to settle down. I can't think of anything worse! I want to be free!'

'Then why the devil did you get engaged to me in the first place!' yelled Tom, his patience exhausted. Corey was so irrational. Only she could rile him like this.

'I thought—I thought, oh, I don't *know*!' It was too long to explain to him. He'd have to be content thinking she was capricious.

'Corey, I want to marry you,' he began.

She pushed the ring into his pocket. 'Rubbish! I zip up your life a bit. Can you ever see me as a high class executive's wife?' She held out her soiled skirts, then slightly pulled at the top of her dress in mock seduction and he laughed, despite himself. She always had that ability to puncture situations.

'Tom, I mean it,' she said, serious again.

'You're unforgettable,' he sighed, 'I was the envy of every man who saw us together.'

'But you must have wondered what you were doing some times?' prompted Corey, and he grinned, nodding.

'I did. It was madness, but a lovely madness. You're so incredible, it made up for the doubts.'

'I won't change. I'd ruin your life,' she said quietly.'

'What a lovely ruin,' he remarked wryly.

She gave a slow smile. 'I'm not going back in there. I'll go out through the garden. Tell them anything you like. Please, I know it's unfair, but I can't face them, especially the big Tycoon. He already thinks I'm the village idiot. Say goodbye nicely, Tom.'

'Goodbye nicely, Tom,' he said obediently.

'*Now* he shows me a sense of humour,' she said, rolling her eyes dramatically.

'You won't go out of my life, will you? Let me take you out sometimes.'

'Maybe. No strings though. Now, give my love to your father and apologies to your mother. Though she'll be delighted to get rid of me. Go *on*!' She stopped his protest with a sisterly finger on his lips. ''Bye, Tom.'

He paused. 'See you later,' he said automatically.

Her hysterical giggle followed his retreating back and, relieved beyond words, she kicked off the restricting shoes, twirling round and round the billiard table lawn in the soft glowing moonlight, executing a wild, joyous dance, bending her lithe body in quick, supple movements. Her eyes glazed, her mouth curved in delight as she spun on slender brown legs, swirling her skirt with one hand, the other thrust jauntily on one hip. Her massed hair flew so fast about her head that it whipped and stung her high raw cheekbones, and the two earrings in her left ear, one a slender silver triangle, the other a snake coil, tinkled lightly so she held her breath to hear them more clearly.

The dance became slower, more sensuous and languid. It was a dance of primitive animal grace, unlearnt, as natural to her as walking.

Finally exhausted, she sank in a breathless heap to the lawn. The dance and the finality of her decision that evening combined with the wine to leave her limp and woolly-headed. It was while she was wondering idly whether the grass stains would ever come out of her white dress that she realised she was not alone. Someone was clapping.

'A very exciting performance,' said Jude drily.

Corey scrambled to her feet, adjusting the neckline which had slipped farther than even she thought decent.

'It was a private one,' she retorted stiffly.

His eyes had watched her hands with avid interest. 'Yes. Amazing how drink takes some women. Maybe you should have followed the ladies.'

'Huh!' scorned Corey. 'I don't follow people.'

'No?'

'Hell fire!' she yelled. 'I keep my freedom!'

'Is freedom so important to you?' he enquired.

'Yes, yes, *yes*!' she answered. 'You can keep all your stuffy, droning lives. I'm not wasting one second in meaningless routine.'

He laughed softly. 'So you think I'm a drone. At the risk of mixing metaphors, may I remind you that sometimes, wolves run with the sheep.' His eyes glittered.

Corey stopped short, surprised. With that expression, he did look a little—rakish. She threw back her head and laughed delightedly at the discovery but found herself losing balance as the adrenalin of freedom fought with the wine for supremacy.

The next moment, she was clasped in his arms. He held her quite formally with a total stillness, till she regained her equilibrium.

'You're not very safe to let out alone,' he said in glacial tones. 'Haven't you any control?'

'Not a lot,' she said happily. 'I think they dished out all my share to you.' Raising recklessly sparkling eyes, she grinned infectiously at his stern face. 'Poor Mr Radcliffe. You look shocked.'

'Wrong,' he replied shortly. 'Disconcerted. You're a very disconcerting young lady.'

'Thank you,' she said, mockingly demure. 'You can let go of me. The world's stopped whizzing around.'

'It might have for you,' he said obliquely, 'but it hasn't for me.'

His arms slid around her more securely and her pliant body swayed indolently towards him. At that moment she was in love with everyone.

'Temptress,' he murmured, the once cold eyes now charcoal soft.

There was something intrinsically wicked, standing locked in embrace with one's ex-fiancé's boss! Corey twined her slender arms around his tanned neck and parted tantalising lips.

'So be tempted,' she urged gently. 'Or is that terribly ungentlemanly?'

'One of these days you'll tease a man too far,' he muttered.

'Can't wait,' she whispered.

The delicate stroking of her fingers on the nape of his neck seemed to be arousing him more than she had anticipated. He closed his eyes and drew in his breath, reaching up to remove her hands, but she resisted, enjoying the hard strength of his body and hoping to prolong the contact. He did better than that: his hand shot up to hold her chin fast and his lips descended on hers in a very, very thorough kiss.

'Mmmm,' she murmured under his warm, seeking mouth.

'Jude, where are you?' called Lydia's voice from the terrace doors.

As the warmth of his body drew away, Corey felt quite bereft, yearning for its return.

'Don't go,' she breathed.

'My God!' he muttered fiercely. 'I wonder if Tom knows what he's let himself in for. One thing is for sure, Miss Lee—your dinner parties will be sensational if you offer yourself to every principal guest.'

Turning on his heel, he strode rapidly back to the house, as though the very devil was after him.

CHAPTER TWO

IN the heady days that followed, Corey forgot the tingles of excitement that she had felt when Jude had kissed her—and her own abandoned response. To begin with, the memory was strong and enjoyable, especially the unexpectedness of his action and the fact that Tom's boss had defied convention. There was also the pleasure of being kissed by an accomplished expert; Tom couldn't always aim straight, she remembered, giggling.

But the scene in the garden receded with the more immediate delight of total freedom. The fact that the days were hers alone, to spend as she pleased, gave Corey a welcome sense of release. Now, time stretched ahead for her to fill—or not—entirely at the whim of her impulses. *That* was exciting!

She had dragged a heavy gas cylinder on to the front path and sat in the glorious summer sun, wielding the blow-torch as she created a silver necklace of butterfly orchids for a silver wedding anniversary present. As the solder ran in a pale silver stream down the final join she sat back, satisfied, waiting till the quenching process was completed and she could give the necklace a final rinse. A warm, contented glow spread through her.

Leaning back in the high swivel chair, she feasted her eyes on the surging colour all around: poppies, delphiniums, larkspur, Sweet Sultan, Love-in-the-mist, Dutchman's breeches ... all a magnet for the busy insect life and a nearby source of nectar for her

31

bees in the orchard.

Life was more pleasant than she had ever known.
Every day, the sleek cat sunned itself on the warm
flagstones, occasionally twining around her legs to
remind her that it was feeding time. They ate when
hungry and slept when tired. In between, Corey
worked for sheer joy in a burst of released creativity.

Since her training at the Sir John Cass School of
Art, and a subsequent short apprenticeship in Hatton
Garden, she had found no lack of orders from London
jewellers. Now she was working almost exclusively on
commissions for a jeweller who was known for his
individual work—and, fortunately, for his under-
standing of creative artists.

One afternoon that June she became drowsy in the
heat, abandoning the cottage garden and curling up in
an armchair to sleep. When the sun eventually set, she
prepared a Julienne soup, using fresh vegetables from
the garden, and popped two tins of well-risen bread
dough into the Aga. After the candlelit supper, and
well gorged on hot crusty bread, she read herself to
sleep, then woke wide awake and suddenly sleepless in
the early hours.

'Hey, Cat,' she confided, as they both stretched
luxuriously, 'how about a moonlight stroll?'

Cat merely flicked his tail and curled up into a
black, glossy circle. Corey slid out of bed, her naked
body gleaming in the bluish light. There were no
curtains at the windows, since she loved to see the
night sky and felt no lack of privacy since the nearest
inhabitants lived at the Manor. As far as she was
concerned, Radcliffe and his ilk were more than a
world away!

It was almost full moon; no need to light a candle.
From her wall cupboard, Corey found a thin cotton

shift to pull over her nakedness. Barefooted, she padded across the creaking floorboards and slipped downstairs and into the cool, still night air. Deliberately she brushed her legs against the herbs edging the path, and bent down to bruise the wild garlic between thumb and forefinger, so that she could inhale its sharp aroma.

In Sedge Wood she ran silently, as her mother had taught her, to the ferny glade. There she waited to hear the nightingale. Every year he came, building his nest, claiming his territory and singing his heart out to the world.

A cold shiver ran across her back at his first plaintive notes, then she sat motionless, listening to the clear, heart-stopping song, ringing joy into her contented mind. This was how she wanted to live: free from all encumbrances.

But in amongst the high-pitched call and the gentle rustlings, another sound intruded. Close by, she heard a crunch of feet and she held her breath, pressing a trembling hand over her thudding heart. Stealthily she reached out and picked up a large piece of wood, standing with her back to a large oak, a fierce expression belying her inner apprehension.

The tall figure of Jude Radcliffe stepped from the shadows into the glade.

'I surrender,' he whispered dramatically, eyeing the heavy stick. 'Do what you will with me!'

Releasing a peal of delighted laughter, Corey flung away the stick, disturbing the wary forest life. Startled noises in the undergrowth on all sides of them indicated frantic bids for freedom in the animal world.

'Oh,' came his disappointed voice. 'Aren't you going to beat me?'

'Idiot!' What an unpredictable man he was! 'I never

knew tycoons went in for that kind of thing.'

'Neither did I till just now. The idea of a nymph flogging me with a chunk of wood in the middle of the night never appealed before.' He leaned lazily against the trunk of a tree and folded his arms. 'It could be the prelude to some erotic occult ritual if we tried hard enough.'

Corey ignored his invitation. 'I'm listening to the nightingale,' she explained.

'With a chunk of wood?'

His amazed, slanting eyebrows made her chuckle helplessly and she sank to the ground, eyes dancing in amusement, his deep, rich laugh echoing through the trees. I like this man, she thought. He's got my off-beat sense of humour.

'I was defending myself,' she answered. 'Most people prowling through the woods at night are up to no good. Why are you here?'

He considered her thoughtfully before joining her. 'I was unsettled. Knowing nothing of nightingales, I merely opted for a walk. Tell me, do nightingales sing in captivity?' His shadowy eyes probed hers.

'Of course not. Haven't you heard Hans Christian Andersen's story?' she asked. 'I wouldn't sing if I was caged.'

'What do we wolves know of you nightingales?' he murmured, 'except that you don't have enough feathers on you. You're cold.'

With surprise, she noticed the raised flesh on her arms.

'Here, take my jacket.'

With a flamboyant gesture, he shrugged it off and handed it to her, refraining from helping her into it.

The lining was slippery satin and slid easily over her bare arms. There was a strange intimacy in wearing the jacket, still warm from his body, and she sucked in her breath slightly, surprised at the glow that surged boldly inside her.

'Warmer?' He was leaning too close, his lashes too seductive as his eyes lowered.

'Much. How silly do I look?'

'Pretty silly. I prefer you in see-through cotton myself.'

There was something dangerously serious underlying his banter. Those eyes of his were saying more than his words pretended. Corey jumped up. 'Want to see a badger set?' she asked.

'If that's all the sights on offer,' he replied.

Briskly she turned to the narrow, well-trodden path at the western end of the glade, walking blithely along, recognising tracks and signs, picking up the musky scent of a fox and revelling in the serenity that surrounded them. Jude trailed along behind her, seemingly fascinated, noticing the obvious and missing more subtle and interesting sights. She smiled to herself, not attempting to detract from his pleasure. He really was a townie!

At one point, he stopped and crouched down.

'Hey! I think I've found some paw prints. Could be a badger,' he called excitedly.

His rapt face pleased her. Odd that. He was, after all, just an ignorant tycoon.

'No,' she said, examining the muddy area beside the path. 'Badgers have five toes. That's a fox. Can you smell it? By the way he was walking, he was after something. He was stalking his prey.'

'Oh, sure,' he said with scepticism.

'Really,' insisted Corey. 'Small, tiptoeing prints, close together. It was creeping along after something.'

'I do believe you're right. How do you know such

things?' he asked in admiration.

Woodcraft was one of the first skills I was taught, she thought to herself.

'You pick that sort of thing up in the country,' she answered, and walked on quickly. 'See this beech tree?' He followed her finger which pointed to a huge beech, scored by deep vertical scars to the height of his waist.

'That's their scratching tree. There's the set.' Her finger swung to a dark hole beneath tangled tree roots.

'I've never seen badgers,' he breathed.

'Good lord, what you tycoons do miss,' teased Corey. 'I'll bring you here some time. You'll have to sit perfectly still for hours though. Could you manage that?'

'With you? I'm not sure.' He grinned. 'Look, if the badgers have gone to ground, how about coffee in my kitchen to round off the tour?'

Corey hesitated. She *did* want to prolong this night.

'Just coffee,' he said confidently, willing to promise anything to hold this elusive nightingale in his hands for a while.

'Done!'

Happily, she reached for his hand and began to run. They raced through the wood, her bare feet making no sound. The rush of air through her hair was exhilarating. Ducking under low branches and jumping over imaginary ones on the path, she whooped loudly, scattering with finality any wildlife in the vicinity. Snatching her hand from his, she leaped into the air for the sheer hell of it and whirled around, panting as he slid to a halt. A strange, rather frightening light shone in his eyes and she moved backwards till she felt the bars of the meadow gate grating roughly against the back of the jacket.

Suddenly she felt vulnerable and underdressed.

'Race you to . . .' She was stopped by the expression on his face as he reached out and put his hands around her waist, inside the jacket. '. . . the house,' she breathed weakly, shaken by the closeness of him and the potential escalation of the situation. The night, her elation and the promise of his eyes filled her with breathtaking excitement.

'Let's race to heaven first,' he murmured.

'No, thanks,' she replied, forcing a strength into her words. 'I've just escaped from one cage. I'm not getting into another.'

'Mmmm. You're speaking of ditching Tom?' His hand pushed up the sleeve of the jacket in an attempt to find her hand and he examined the third finger. It was now ringless. 'After succumbing to your charms that night, I felt very ashamed of my behaviour and was relieved to hear Tom's news. It explained your behaviour too, of course. But,' he added, slipping his arms around to the inward curve of her back, 'I wasn't planning to cage you. I thought we'd fly around together for a while. Soar into the sky and do a few aerobatics, that sort of thing.'

'I see. Thanks for the invitation, but I'd rather you stayed on the ground and I flew alone. You see, I don't do things by half measures; with me, it's all or nothing and you've come at the wrong time for it to be all.'

Jude held her at arm's length and stared at her. 'Was Tom *all*?'

'What has that got to do with you?' she defied.

'Was he?'

'Make up your own mind.'

'You're inexperienced, that I gathered from our kiss.'

'Well!' Corey was affronted. Hadn't he been

stunned by her response in Tom's garden? It had
certainly stunned her! What an analytical man he was
to assess her. No doubt the fair Lydia had a very good
technique. A pang shot through Corey's body.

'Not everyone has your extensive experience,' she
said tartly. 'For a start, I'm much younger than you,'
she grinned inwardly as Jude winced, 'and for another
thing, I don't go around kissing every Dick and Harry.
Only Tom. And one or two before him. I may be
inexperienced by your standards, but not anyone
else's.'

'You fooled me with your innocence, then. Perhaps
Tom didn't take the relationship very far; maybe he
was the cautious one.'

At that, Corey flamed red. His remark was too close
to the truth. She had been eager enough; Tom had
displayed a surprising reluctance to make love to her.
He wanted his wife to be a virgin and he had taken
elaborate precautions to ensure that they were rarely
alone in tempting situations; he had discovered
Corey's quick passion was easy to ignite once she
trusted someone and he was hardly immune to her
sensuality.

'Unbelievable!' muttered Jude. 'Good God, the
man's a fool!' He pulled her close again and whispered
in her ear, lightly massaging the back of her neck with
one hand. 'Any normal man would want you. There's
something healthily earthy about the way you move,
the way you look at a man. Corey, did you want to
make love to him?'

'Are you the kind of man who gets his kicks from
hearing about other people's relationships?' she
retorted. 'It's definitely no business of yours. Let's

change the subject. Talking about sex is exciting you too much.'

Jude gripped her hard, angry at her forthright manner. 'Why, you . . .'

'We were going to have some coffee, remember?' interrupted Corey. 'I'm still cold.'

He smiled wryly. 'You, cold?'

'My outside is.'

'I'm trying to warm you up.'

'I'd prefer coffee.'

'Very well.' Swiftly he changed position and lifted her in his arms, fumbling with the latch on the gate. 'Why, Miss Lee, I do believe you're wearing nothing but your skin under this flimsy cotton!' His hand crept slowly around her body towards her breast. Corey wriggled, succeeding only in twisting her skirt up to her thighs.

'More, more,' he murmured, laughing and sending rivulets of warmth diving through her veins.

'Oh, damn you! Why do men always assume their attentions are welcomed? Stop groping!' She buried her head in his shirt and tried to take a bite of his chest.

'You wild-cat!' He set her down. 'You're certainly no nightingale. Come on then, we'll walk decently to the house and discuss your payment.' On he strode, leaving her to run after him.

'What payment?' she demanded.

'For damages to my horse, and for trespass on my land. *And* there's tonight's trespass to take into account.'

'You bastard! Old Mr Wallace always let me roam the wood.'

'I bet. He had something of a penchant for gipsies like you.'

Corey flinched and grew white.

'What's the matter?' asked Jude, steadying her.

'Nothing,' she answered guardedly.

He gave a swift frown and attempted to put his arm around her waist, but she slipped from his friendly embrace and hurried on ahead.

'You know the way?' he asked, as she turned on to the path that led to the Manor's huge kitchen.

'I lived here once.'

'Yes, I know you did. Not by name. Father and I knew he'd taken in a girl to work in the house.'

'You knew him, then?' Corey was surprised. She'd never heard Mr Wallace talk of a Jude Radcliffe.

'I'll tell you all about our relationship. Come in and all will be revealed.'

'Spare me *that* sir,' she cried, with an arch look that set them both laughing. How quick he was to appreciate her gently acidic remarks! Often people found her meanings obscure. She relaxed and stepped into the old-fashioned room, but was astonished to see that someone had redesigned the kitchen, replacing the ugly old units with beautiful natural pine.

'This is lovely,' she murmured, running her hands over the satisfyingly silky wood finish. She opened a cupboard: thick natural wood, easy swing, well-designed hinges—quality stuff!

Someone liked flowers, too. There were massive bunches of Peace roses, some just a little overblown and spilling faded yellow petals on to the bleached-wood work surfaces.

'What do you think?' asked Jude cautiously. 'Before you say anything in your frank way, I'd better tell you that I chose this style.'

'I love it. You've put a lot of care into this.'

'Yes,' he said drily. 'And a lot of cash.'

Corey tipped her head on one side and tried to work out his probable investment. 'I couldn't have bought the units in here, let alone the whole estate.'

'Well, I didn't buy it,' he said, removing a bottle of wine from the fridge. 'Help yourself to cheese. Old Mr Wallace, as you call him, was my uncle-in-law. My aunt died in childbirth, the child too. He left me the house, virtually commanding me to renovate it and conserve the flora and fauna around.' He grinned at her. 'That included you.'

'Me?'

'He said, "Look after the fairy at the bottom of my garden."'

She bit into the crusty bread with her sharp white teeth. 'Don't make fun of me,' she complained, speaking through a mouthful of crumbs. 'He didn't say that.'

'You want to see the will? I was specifically asked to keep an eye on you. Father and I always wondered about your relationship with him.'

'He didn't fancy me, if that's what you're insinuating. But he . . .' Corey remembered his concern. 'He took me under his wing,' she finished lamely. She'd been a substitute daughter to Newton, she knew that.

'Really.' Jude didn't sound convinced. Too bad. He'd have to make do with her explanation—she was damned if she was going to tell him the whole story.

'It's silly, him asking you to watch out for me. Good Lord! As if I needed fathering!'

She perched on the edge of the worktop and watched him spreading Camembert, thick and creamy, on his bread.

'You have a father around?' he asked curiously.

'No.' Her face darkened and she scowled, sliding off the top and exposing the long slender length of her legs.

'Dead?' he asked more gently.

'None of your business,' she snapped. 'I hate people prying. If you only got me in here to ask questions, I'm going.'

As she stalked tautly to the door, he caught her arm and swung her around, staring at her blazing eyes.

'I'm sorry if I touched a raw nerve,' he said softly. 'I won't pry. Don't leave yet. You'll never sleep with all that cheese inside you.'

Despite herself, Corey laughed at him, her mouth arching to show those dazzling teeth. His eyes narrowed and his hands slid possessively up her arms.

'You promised just coffee,' she complained, unable to prevent the huskiness of desire. His touch was setting her aflame. 'I didn't expect the Inquisition and a pass as well.'

'No? Well, I lied to you. I wanted more than coffee.' He ran his finger around her parted mouth, his gaze intent. She responded immediately, snatching at his finger with sharp teeth, arching her body like a cat and closing those glowing eyes in rapture.

'I'm not sure whether you are artless or totally calculating,' he whispered.

'I don't calculate anything. I just react,' breathed Corey.

'Then react to this.' In one movement, he slid his hands around the curve of her back to hold her fast, and simultaneously surrounded her parted lips with his firm mouth, the warm moistness of it sending a sudden shock racing through her body. Tantalisingly, his fingers trailed down her back, then with a muttered exclamation he roughly tore the jacket from her shoulders and she was pulled violently against the length of his body.

Weakness invaded her, leaving her head spinning. Pliant to his desire, she dragged his head down harder on to her mouth, clutching blindly at his thick warm hair. Within her burned a raging need that she had never before experienced. His lips softened into light, feathering kisses, which sent tiny quivers of heat coursing into her womb.

Reeling from his unexpected onslaught, she gave in to the wonderful floating feeling that flowed through her like dark red wine. If only she could surrender utterly to the sensation, like a healthy animal! She adored being touched, being kissed like this.

'Hey,' murmured Jude's voice in her ear, brushing the lobe with his warm breath, 'you're not concentrating. You can't frown when I'm kissing you.'

Corey began to protest, only to find her mouth once more claimed by Jude's lips, but this time they forced harder, roaming more fiercely, and he groaned softly as she clung to him, her curves straining into his hard body. His relentless kisses grew more exploratory, making her skin hum as his moist lips moved around her jawline and down to the soft, dark hollow of her throat. She tipped her head back, the black glossy waterfall of her hair flowing down her back, knowingly inviting him with her abandoned posture.

He became very still, only his laboured breathing betraying his passion.

'Do you know what you're doing?' he whispered.

Slowly, Corey tipped her head forwards again, her lips formed into a sighing pout. The wild storm in her head subsided, her pulse steadied. Her responses had let her down again. Arousal always flared too quickly—but there was a reason why she felt so abandoned, of course, it was part of her nature.

This was different; how, she wasn't sure. Warning bells rang in her mind—bells that threatened a headlong involvement. For it wasn't just Jude's touch that excited her immeasurably, it was an attraction that went beyond sensuality. The mental rapport between them was special and she had to decide whether to fan the flames or damp them down. Jude would take away from her the recently won control she had gained over her life, she recognised that.

She lowered her hooded eyes and took a step back, pushing hard against his heaving chest. He released her and she stood, awkwardly twisting the material of her skirt.

'I'm sorry. I got carried away. I'm odd at night.' She gave a nervous laugh. 'Tom says—said—I was a creature of the night. It affects me. Especially when there's a new moon.'

'There isn't one tonight.' Jude's voice was flat and toneless. He obviously didn't believe in helping her to escape from her passions with dignity.

'Well, there ought to be!' she retorted. 'And don't think you've scored, Jude Radcliffe, because you haven't. I just enjoy being kissed and you do it very well, as you probably know. But now I feel embarrassed, so perhaps you'd let me roam the woods in peace and leave me alone in future. I want to get on with my own life without men invading it ten times a minute!'

Jude said nothing.

'Stop looking at me like that,' she said sharply.

'I'm trying to work you out,' he replied. 'I can't think how Tom coped with your waywardness.'

'Don't bother. I'm erratic. Ask Tom. I won't fit any pattern you know. I liked your cheese, thanks.' She ran to the door.

'My cheese . . .!' laughed Jude incredulously, as she reached for the latch.

'Good night,' she answered, giggling to herself at his amazement.

Jude strode to the window and watched the slender white form run lightly over the field, clamber with ease over the gate and disappear like a wraith into the wood. Good night indeed! He shook his head wryly. No wonder Uncle Newton had wanted someone to look after his protégée. She was too honest and too wild for her own good, an enchanting cross between a woman and a child. Someone ought to take her in hand, someone who would not take advantage of that open nature, who would give her all the freedom she wanted and guide her through life. God, he was sounding pretentious! Corey made him more and more aware of his acquired clichés. He'd no idea how stylised he'd become.

Jude tidied away the midnight picnic they had shared. There couldn't be many men who could handle her. He was damned if *he* could. And yet . . . He supposed most men found her fascinating—he was no exception. Could she be as innocent as she seemed? Her reactions to his passes had been instant, as if she saw sex as a natural part of her life. Perhaps her unpractised response to him had more to do with the inadequacy of her lovers than a lack of them. How many of them had held her eager body as he had? How many, more unscrupulous, had taken advantage of her wanton response? And why, for God's sake, hadn't he pressed home his advantage?

He kicked the fridge door shut, suddenly angry. Damnation! The woman had mesmerised him. He wandered aimlessly around the kitchen, picking things up and putting them down again. Now that she was gone, everything seemed empty and dull: his business meeting in London tomorrow had lost its former attraction. He wanted to be here, with Corey, finding out more about her, talking to her, sharing time with her. There was some unusual skeleton in her cupboard, that was for sure. She was hiding something in her past that made her shy away like a frightened colt.

Just as well really. He hadn't the time nor the inclination to become involved with a girl as mercurial and naturally feckless as he had once been.

Into his mind flashed the image of Catalina, the dark-eyed woman who had hurt him so much. Corey could easily disturb his future, just as Catalina had destroyed his past. Jude walked thoughtfully up the stairs. The tug of war between sense and senses had begun.

It was equally unsettling for Corey, having had her passions stirred so sublimely. Jude Radcliffe had managed to spice up her night prowl more than she bargained for. All night she fidgeted, till Cat walked out of her bedroom to find a more peaceful place to sleep.

'It's all right for you, Cat,' she grumbled, 'no one minds if you slope off in the night and indulge in a bit of carnal pleasure. Wish I was a cat too.'

Black coffee kept her tolerably awake the next day and she concentrated on simple box rings, leaving the finer work for a day when she was less agitated. But the simplicity of the jobs left her too much time for thinking. Only rarely had she ever considered her actions in advance. It took something momentous, like continued ridicule or a period of depression, to force her into plans for the future. Too often she ran her life in headstrong spontaneity. Jude Radcliffe was one gorgeous hunk of man and she might have indulged herself—but oh, the pleasure of independence! No man could offer that! He was the last man she needed at this time.

And, having decided that Tom was too upper-crust for her to cope with, she could hardly contemplate a relationship with the Radcliffe millions! Every time she looked at him, she'd be thinking about artichokes. And napkins. Or was it serviettes? It would waste her life, worrying about such things.

Anyway, she had crushed physical needs before; she could do it again. The invasion of her mind was a different matter. She smiled, remembering their woodland meeting.

Damn! She'd dropped the pliers. Ducking under the portable workbench, she reached for them and found her fingers a few inches from a pair of walking boots.

How odd she hadn't heard: she must have been unusually engrossed. Cat had retreated to the cottage door and stood with arched back and fluffed out tail, growling quietly.

'Yes?' she asked warily, bending a silver oblong till the ends met. The man followed her movements carefully. He wasn't a hiker. Too sure of himself.

'Miss Lee?'

'Who wants her?' She reached for the borax cone and made up a paste, spreading a thin line along the join for the solder to run. Looking up, she found the man watching intently.

'I do. I'm Jack Spurr, estate manager for

Sedgewood Manor. What are you doing?' he asked curiously.

Corey turned on the gas jet. 'Soldering.'

The borax fluffed up and simmered down again as she heated each side of the ring.

'Do you work indoors with that?' He pointed to the gas cylinder.

'I'm hardly going to sit out here when it rains, am I?' she asked mildly.

'I see.' He took out a notebook and wrote quickly.

'How do my actions concern you?' she asked.

'I'm investigating Sedgewood property. You live in this lodge house free of rent, I gather.'

'Mr Wallace said I could.' Corey was suddenly anxious. 'Surely Tycoon Radcliffe isn't going to cast me out into the snow?'

'Mr Radcliffe might have to re-consider your tenancy, after I write my report,' countered the manager. 'However, if you do have to leave, it'll be well before snow sets in.'

What a stolid, humourless man he was! She tipped her head on one side, eyeing him critically. Was he worth wheedling? The house-martins dived past her ear, en route for the nest under the thatch, and she knew she didn't want to be pushed out of her home—not yet, anyway.

'Would you like some tea?' she asked, wide-eyed and sweetly innocent.

'No, thanks. I need to see the house, though.'

Politely, she pushed wide the latch door and he poked around her neat living room, taking in the clean chintz covers, the pine table and chairs and the blue Spode set on the old dresser. Everything was spotless.

He was astonished to discover she had no kitchen and no bathroom, nor electricity. He wrote furiously, then looked up from his notebook.

'I'm pretty certain you're operating illegally, running a business from here. I assume it's a business.' He ran his eye over the neatly addressed parcels and the racks of saws and chisels on the wall. 'Also, you can't use that gas in the house—and probably not outside it. Not with that thatch.'

'What! Everyone's always known what I do here. Mr Wallace . . .'

'Time doesn't stand still,' began Jack Spurr.

'It does here,' claimed Corey wildly.

'Not now Mr Radcliffe has taken over. This cottage is in his possession now,' cut in the manager curtly. 'You'll be hearing from us about the rent and the operation of the cylinder.'

Silenced, Corey waited while he ducked his head under the low door and disappeared down her path. Radcliffe couldn't throw her out on a technicality—could he?

In a sudden flash of inspiration, she ran towards her boundary hedge, thought better of it, returned to fill a basket with honey, freshly baked bread and tiny peas picked that morning, then scrambled through the thornless briar and on to Manor land. She wasn't above a little gentle corruption when it suited her.

To her dismay, Jude was just greeting Lydia, who had turned up in a white Lotus Elan. From all the continental kissing going on, Lydia was a regular visitor now. She sighed. Oh well, there wasn't much point in playing the waif-and-stray-turned-out-of-house-and-home now, not with Lydia around. She toyed with the idea of running up to Jude Radcliffe and flinging herself at his feet in some kind of supplication and begging for the roof over her head, but even she decided that was a little over the top.

With reluctance, she trailed back to the cottage, wondering whether it was just the anxiety of losing her home and place of work, or whether it was the sight of Jude's tall form bending over Lydia's immaculate blonde head that made her so depressed.

'Hi, Cat,' she said listlessly, dumping her basket on the floor. With a lithe spring, Cat landed on her lap and curled up contentedly. 'Glad someone loves me,' she muttered, and unaccountably, her eyes began to fill with tears. 'Oh dear!' she moaned, tipping off Cat as she jumped up in confusion. 'What on earth's the matter with me?'

Corey wandered around aimlessly, then decided to wash her hair and have a bath. First she pumped up the water and set every saucepan she possessed on the stove to heat. Using some of the water she washed her hair in the bowl, then, by the time the saucepans had been refilled and were boiling merrily away for her bath, it was quite dark outside.

Her black, feathered hair dripped down her naked back as she padded backwards and forwards to the tub with the steaming saucepans until the water reached the bright yellow wavy line which she had painted on the inside.

She stepped into the water and slid carefully into a sitting position, hugging her knees to her chin and closing her eyes, squeezing them tightly so that she could feel the long lashes brushing her cheeks.

How long she stayed like that, emptying her mind in an attempt to clear her emotions, she did not know. But when she opened her eyes again the water was cold and someone was knocking at the door.

'Damn!' she muttered, searching for the towel. 'Where ... oh, Cat! What are you doing!' she said affectionately, seeing that he had dragged the towel close to the Aga and was contentedly curled in its folds.

The knocking grew louder and as Corey tiptoed across to retrieve the towel, she became aware of Jude's voice outside.

'Corey! Answer! Are you all right? Corey! Are you in . . .'

Corey unceremoniously hauled up the towel, tipping Cat on to the floor. He let out a furious yowl and Jude burst in.

'What's the . . . my God!'

His smoky eyes travelled hotly down her slender body, resting on the small up-tilted breasts, hard-tipped from the chill of the bath.

The message in his darkened eyes was unmistakable. Its blazing power created warmth in her veins even as his gaze lifted to her face. Corey twisted the towel around her like a sari and ran her fingers through her wet hair.

'It's a bit like the movies,' she said huskily.

'What do you mean?' Jude's voice was shaky.

'Girl has message from bailiff to quit, Lord of Manor enters, "Aha, maiden, be mine or else!"'

He grinned, relaxing. 'It's nothing like that, I can assure you. Well, that wasn't my original intention. However,' he examined her legs carefully, 'I like the idea.'

Corey backed away and Jude smiled.

'Trouble is, you couldn't have much of a satisfying chase round this room, could you?' he said innocently, glancing around the small space.

Despite her uncertainty, the corners of Corey's mouth lifted. 'I'll set my cat on you,' she threatened.

'I'm terrified,' he drawled, looking pointedly at the animal curving sinuous patterns around his legs and purring loudly. 'What's his name?'

'Cat.'

'Original.'

'He doesn't like anyone but me.'

Jude bent down and Cat sprang on to his broad shoulder to nuzzle his ear.

'So I see. While he's murdering my ear lobe, can I sit down? I've had a hard day.'

'I'm sure you have,' she said tartly, remembering Lydia.

'Oh, we Lords of the Manor do work, you know. That's how we become Lords. Look,' he said, arranging himself comfortably in the large chintz armchair, 'I'm sorry about Spurr—my manager. He's damn efficient and I had no idea he'd made so much progress around the estate. I was going to speak to him about you before he came.'

'Indeed. Well, before we discuss that, would you mind going upstairs and finding me something to wear? Take five minutes to do that and I'll be vaguely dry by then.'

'What's wrong with your legs making the journey? They look eminently . . . er . . . supple to me.'

'It'll be cold up there—I always leave the windows wide open. I prefer to dry by the stove. And if I go up those stairs, virtually above your head, you'll be seeing more than you ought.'

Jude chuckled. 'Very sound reasons. See you in a few minutes.'

With a thumping heart, Corey rapidly dried herself, rubbing fiercely with the rough towel till her flawless olive skin glowed a dusky pink. All the time she faced the stairs, watching and listening, but he seemed to be quietly sitting up there, perhaps on her bed.

'I'm ready. Where's my clothes?' she called.

An arm appeared, waving her favourite faded crimson skirt and what looked like the black vest T-shirt. Corey grabbed them, then frowned.

'Is that all?'

'Didn't think you wore underclothes,' he shouted.

'Well, I do. Sometimes,' she said petulantly. None of his business what she wore! It wasn't right that anyone else should know what she liked to do in the summer.

'I'm coming down,' he said firmly.

Rot him! She'd have to wear what he'd chosen. Corey was disconcerted to see how much her breasts thrust against the thin cotton jersey of the T-shirt. She rubbed her warm hands over the swelling nipples in an attempt to soften them but for some reason that only made them harder. She curled up in the basket chair and folded her arms as Jude appeared.

'Hmm, very fetching,' he drawled, claiming the chintz again. 'I'm sorry I couldn't come earlier. Though if I had, what a treat I would have missed! It's not every day you see nightingales in their natural habitat, splashing about in their little baths.'

He looked so relaxed, so much at home in her little room. He ought to have been out of place, being so used to elegant drawing rooms, but he wasn't. He was quite a lad, entertaining one woman in the afternoon and flirting with another in the evening. She must remember how casual he was and keep him at arm's length this time.

'Fun, isn't it, happening on quaint country customs,' she said sarcastically. 'Maybe it will increase your fun if you empty the bath for me.'

'Of course. Where?' He looked around the room.

'Outside,' Corey told him. 'By the pump there's a soak-hole.'

'Oh, very rural,' he muttered, and dragged the tin bath to the door.

It was a relief to have him out of the room for a moment. The air was charged with overpowering sexual tension. Despite the light conversation, there was an underlying crackling current flowing between them both. And I'm not having electricity in this place! thought Corey, amused at her own wit.

'Would you like some coffee?' she asked when he returned, turning for safety to social ritual.

'Thanks, that'll be fine. Tell me, what's that overpowering perfume I can smell outside? It wasn't your bathwater.'

'Honeysuckle, night-scented stock, lemon balm—do you want a list? It'll take ages. I planted pungent herbs and flowers round the garden path. That way, every time I walk along it I get a good sniff of them.'

She brought over the coffee and he stretched out his long legs. Cat clambered up on to his chest, resting his chin against Jude's collar bone, perfectly at ease.

'You know about plants, do you?' He actually sounded interested.

'Can't you tell?' She waved a hand at the flowers hanging to dry, the dried herbs in bunches: tansy, feverfew, betony; the great bowls of foxgloves, rosebay willowherb and crab-apple.

He grinned sheepishly. 'I didn't honestly notice. There were other, more exciting distractions. How knowledgeable are you?'

She shrugged. 'I don't know what you mean. I revamped the cottage garden when I arrived a few years ago and set up the herb garden, pruned back the fruit trees and so on. My ... my mother knew all about plants and taught me.'

'I was talking to one of my designers this afternoon; she suggested a formal herb garden by the kitchen and we both thought that all the lodges should show a riot of colour in country garden style—something like yours. Spurr tells me this cottage has a real old-fashioned garden. How about giving some advice to my staff on the plants that grow well here? It would take a hell of a load from my landscape designer's shoulders; he's still trying to sort out the Florida end.'

'I don't have the expertise,' she began.

'You could stay here then, rent free,' he suggested craftily.

'Rent free?' she queried.

'Yes. This place is so lacking in facilities that I couldn't accept rent.'

'I wasn't going to offer any,' she said drily.

'We'd modernise the cottage for you, put in . . .'

'No! I don't want it!' Corey jumped up and stood with her hands clenched at the very idea. 'This cottage stays as it is if I'm in it.'

'You are a strange girl,' Jude said softly. 'O.K., sit down. Have it as you want. Will you take on the job?'

How tempting it all was. She and Newton Wallace had spent hours re-designing the gardens of Sedgewood, though their plans were only dreams. Still, she knew exactly how she wanted the lodges to look, and the herb garden. But how wise was it to increase the amount of contact she had with Jude Radcliffe?

CHAPTER THREE

'I'VE got my commissions,' Corey said slowly, torn between her work and the pleasure of seeing the lodge gardens in bloom again—and of having a part in their creation.

'Commissions? Is that anything to do with dangerous gas cylinders my manager was telling me about? You repair them, or something?'

She laughed. 'I'm a tin basher. Silversmith,' she added at Jude's puzzled face.

'That explains the inordinate amount of files and pointed things on your desk,' he said.

'It's a work-bench. Look,' she caught his hand and drew him up. 'The wood's cut away in a curve so you can sit tight into the bench and this leather attached to it acts as a kind of apron. That way, when you file, or if you drop any silver, it gets caught in the leather and doesn't go into the cracks in the tiles.'

'And this,' he said, picking up a heavy oblong pendant, 'this is your design, your work?'

'Yes. Do you like it?'

Jude turned the pendant in his hands. It was three-dimensional, with tiny, billowing clouds at the top and a carved cornfield below. Tall red-gold poppies mingled with white-gold ears of wheat.

'It's fantastic,' he breathed. 'You're very talented, very creative. I had no idea . . .'

'Oh!' she blushed at his praise.

Two lean hands grasped her arms. 'You, blushing? The off-beat, quick-tongued child of nature blushing?

Surely only staid, pure young maidens do that?' Though his tone was teasing, Corey intuitively sensed that he really was seeing her in a different light. His hands, as they slid up her arms, were gentle, his eyes soft and caring.

She pulled away quickly, feeling suddenly trapped. Jude lowered his eyes and bit his lip.

'Sorry,' he said. 'My mistake.'

Puzzled, Corey turned and picked up Cat, busying herself by stroking his silky ears. The importance of his opinion disconcerted her. Why should she care so much what he thought?

'What about the gardens?' asked Jude gently.

Corey thought about the potential pleasure she would gain. The gardens were so neglected.

'Who do I talk to?' she asked warily.

'I've brought down my head-gardener. He's tidying everything up and marking time till the landscape chappie arrives. Just chat to him, that's all.'

'O.K.,' she agreed. 'I'll do it. I assume I'm now allowed back on Manor land again? You won't sue me, or shout at me?'

Jude's face relaxed, and crinkles appeared around his eyes when he smiled. 'You can come on to my land whenever, however and dressed in whatever you like. Just don't drive through at ninety miles an hour again. Come up to the house tomorrow and we'll have an on-site discussion.'

'Sounds businesslike.'

'It is. Think about your fee. Be ready to bargain. Thanks for the coffee. I'll be around from eight onwards. Turn up any time after.' He smiled briefly and turned to the door, but seemed to forget its height in his hurry to leave and banged his head hard on the lintel.

'Ow!' He doubled up, pressing his hand hard against his forehead.

'Jude! Oh lord—here, sit down,' ordered Corey, startled at his ashen face. Jude's legs buckled and she helped him to lean against the dresser, then reached for a white china pot.

'Take your hand away,' she said briskly. 'Let me see the damage.'

Across his forehead was an angry red weal of broken skin and an area already darkening around it. She dipped the tips of her fingers in the ointment and gently rubbed it in.

'What the hell is that?' he asked, wincing.

'Serpent's tongue,' she said absently.

'Ha ha!'

'No, really.' She grinned at his horrified face. 'The plant, silly. Serpent's tongue leaves, bruised and crushed in olive oil. Good for bruises. And I'll make you some tea to steady you.'

'Rather have whisky,' muttered Jude.

'Valerian tea. Calms nerves. Get off the cold tiles and back into the chair while I do a quick infusion.'

'You're a witch,' he said. 'A real live witch. My head doesn't hurt so much now. What is that magic potion you're mixing for me?'

'What?' She was preoccupied with measuring the tea.

'Is that some kind of aphrodisiac?' he asked suspiciously as she presented him with the fragrant brew.

'No. Why, do you need one?' Corey paused in front of his knees, widening her eyes innocently. Jude swore softly and put the mug on the floor. 'You tantalising creature.' He reached out and pulled her on to his lap. She fitted into him perfectly—too perfectly.

'Don't wriggle, little witch. I'm after the secret of your power.'

'So long as that's all,' she murmured as his lips descended.

His head drew back briefly. 'I make no promises,' he breathed.

Then his mouth had enclosed hers, and she felt as right in his arms as she did in the life she had created in the cottage. She nestled deeply, reaching her hands to his thick brown hair and pressing the back of his head so that his mouth ground against hers. Against the softness of her breasts she could feel his hot hard body and a rapidly beating, drumming heart. Was it his, or hers? She wasn't sure. His kisses deepened, his mouth explored hers softly, then drifted lightly to the soft fleshy lobe of her ear and down to the warm hollow of her throat. She responded by touching the tip—just the tip—of his tongue, with her own.

'I like that,' she murmured without thinking.

Every muscle in his body tensed; he grabbed a handful of her still damp hair and manoeuvred her on to the floor, raising himself above her, his eyes glowing dark slate, his breathing heavy.

Corey flung her arms out sideways, stretching her body like a lithe cat.

'Witch,' he muttered again. 'You're irresistible, Corey.'

He traced the high arch of her lips with his fingers and she caught them once again in her white teeth, gently biting them, staring provocatively at him as she did so.

Gently he let his fingers follow her jaw-line, the curve of her shoulders, and then they were still. It

seemed as though he was trying to control himself.
Corey raised herself on her elbows, ready to cool the
situation—it had gone far enough she realised with a
sudden shock—but the movement was her undoing,
for his hands rested now on the swelling mounds of her
breasts.

'Oh my God!' he breathed, and roughly dragged up
the hem of her T-shirt to expose her breasts, pushing
her back to the floor as he did so. Before she could
evade him, his mouth was working furiously on her
lips, forcing them open, invading, and she was
drowning, dying, moaning from the onslaught, her
body flooding with pleasure waves as his fingers
roused her breasts.

She swam in a hazy throb of pleasure, his fingers,
lips and tongue seemingly everywhere, rousing every
nerve, bringing every part of her skin to life. Never
had she been so aware of her own body, its power to
excite, its power to receive such sensual signals from a
man's caresses. Wildly pushing aside his shirt, she
pressed her palms against his back, revelling in the
smooth muscled planes. Their mouths met, ravaged,
and parted again, seeking further areas to conquer
with their urgent hunger. She could bear it no longer.
Despite the pressure of his legs and thighs, his hands
had not strayed below her waist; she was willing him
to do so now, even while she willed herself to resist
him.

'You're so smooth to touch, like satin,' he breathed,
his lips brushing her shoulder. 'I could touch you for
hours.' He took her head in his hands and kissed her,
deepening the kiss till her head spun in an endless
vortex. 'Let's go upstairs,' he murmured hoarsely in
her ear.

'No, let's not,' she countered desperately. If she

gave in to him, she would commit more than her body.

'Here, then?' He stroked her face softly.

Corey hated denying herself. She groaned. 'Nowhere then.' Her eyes were the colour of dark chocolate. They held his in an intent gaze.

'This is ridiculous,' he grated. 'Surely you're not going to play the tease with me? I thought you weren't like that. I want you. I want to devour every part of your gorgeous body.' His lips were moving seductively over her breasts again and their breathing quickened together. 'I must have you, Corey!'

'You will *not* have me, do you hear?' In her frustration and anguish, she raised her voice. 'It's my body. I decide what I do with it. If you made love to me, you'd think you had some kind of rights over me. And I won't have anyone as my master. I *won't* be had!'

'Oh, no,' he moaned, rolling away and holding his head.

'Jude!' She was instantly contrite. 'Have you got a headache?'

'*No*'! he snapped. 'It seems *you* have!'

He rose unsteadily to his feet, his eyes still drugged with passion when they turned on her.

'Goddamn it, Corey, you carry on like that much more and you'll get yourself raped. Learn to control yourself before you get that far. It's totally unfair. Damn it, it's maddening! Don't you dare lead me on ever again.'

His words frightened her; she clutched at her rumpled top and pulled it down.

'It's too late to do that now,' he grated. 'I've tasted you. What we've done hasn't satisfied me. I want more. I want to possess you.'

They stood in her tiny room, breathing heavily, one

wary, one full of frustrated passion.

'Don't you feel it?' he breathed. 'Don't you feel the sparks between us, the chemistry? Doesn't every part of your body ache with desire?'

'Of course it does,' she said weakly, longing to close the gap between them and let the waves of wanting roll over her once more. 'But I won't be possessed, I won't! The idea terrifies me; not to own myself or my life any more. That's what happened with Tom.'

'But I'm not trying to marry you, Corey.'

'I know. But . . .' She couldn't tell him how, unlike Tom, he was even at this stage invading her mind. If she slept with him, the feeling would be even more intense. He'd take her over, body and soul, she was sure. 'Don't ask me to explain, because I won't. Just accept that there's a reason I feel trapped.'

'But I don't want to trap you,' he said softly.

'You are,' she accused. 'That's how it is with me. When I give myself, that's it, I give everything. Trouble is, I regret it. So I want you to leave. Mind your head as you go out.'

'My head is no longer my own,' he muttered. 'Nor my body, nor my emotions. You seem to have them all. You talk about feeling trapped! How the devil do you think I feel!' His eyes blazed bright. 'Why do you think I'm still unmarried? Don't you know that a man in my position ought to have a wife to help him entertain? I've felt trapped, just like you whenever relationships get heavy. But I've never known such an obsession as the one I have for you, and let me tell you, I resent it! I object to you filling my life when I should be concentrating on business, particularly as you have such enviable independence. It's not funny, Corey, virtually running the working lives of hundreds of people and then discovering that your life is being turned upside-down by a wayward, changeable child!'

'I'm not a child! I'm a woman!' cried Corey.

'You're a child with a woman's body. You want all the pleasures and none of the responsibilities. That's not being adult.'

'Don't you dare lecture me! I'm not one of your lackeys, Jude Radcliffe! You're pretty impetuous and irresponsible yourself, kissing girls you think are engaged and trying to seduce girls in woods and bursting into people's houses while they're having a bath and . . .'

'Oh, for God's sake!' he thundered. 'Grow up, Corey. We've set off something inside each of us that's taking us over. It's no use pretending it's not there. I don't like what's happening any more than you do, but don't deny it. It's something special, Corey, I know.'

'Well, I've heard some good lines in my time, but that's the best!' she cried.

'It's not a "line" as you call it. I mean what I say,' he said quietly.

'You know you're on to a good thing, more like it,' flared Corey angrily. 'Don't you know how much I hate myself for responding to you as I did? I'm not proud that I fell for your skilful manipulation.'

'You've got me all wrong,' he protested.

'You *weren't* trying to seduce me?'

'Of *course* I was trying to seduce you . . .' he began.

'Mr Radcliffe, I said I'd sort out your lodge gardens and I will. But that will be the extent of our relationship. I can't bear to be tucked in someone else's pocket and I can't bear to be out of my class. If I decided to have a fling it wouldn't be with anyone like you. I'd find someone of my own type and a working-class background. So go and take a cold bath, and I promise I won't look in *your* window while you're having it.'

'Damn you, Corey,' he shouted. 'Damn you to hell!'

Shaking with frustration and fury, Jude reached the door in two strides, pushed up the latch and ducked—carefully, very carefully—under the lintel.

The next morning Corey was up very early, feeding the hens and searching for their eggs, determined to make her life return to normality. She found three dark, speckled eggs in favourite nesting sites in the hedge and popped them, still warm, into the egg basket on her arm.

How far removed she was from the Radcliffe way of living! You couldn't go egg-hunting if you were Jude Radcliffe's wife, or his mistress. Or even a girl friend. You'd have to smarten yourself up, have lots of hair-dos, so you'd be ready for a quick trip to London or New York. You couldn't dangle your bare feet in the brook in Sedge Wood. You'd be wearing stockings and well-polished shoes.

Corey fixed a plate of scrambled eggs for herself. To keep her hard-won lifestyle, she must not tangle with Jude. He'd want to alter her, to tame her: men always did. They were very conservative creatures. Better to keep him at a spade's length! Mind you, the way he behaves, she thought, it ought to be a rake's length! And yet she was on her way to meet him again. She must be mad.

It was a long time since she'd first walked up the drive of Sedgewood Manor. A long time since Mr Wallace had taken a paternal interest in her, because, he said, he'd once fallen in love with a gipsy woman. Fresh from a furious row with her mother, who had been pushing her for months to 'find a nice *gaje* husband', Corey found a second home with Newton. He taught her the intricacies of arithmetic and English, marvelling at her rapid progress, and she opened out as he drew from her the pain of being virtually stateless, between two societies.

The villagers, believing her to be a wayward girl who'd run away from home, either condemned their friendship or were fascinated by it. The old man was eccentric, that was generally agreed. He was always taking in tramps and one particular band of gipsies were allowed to camp on his land in the summer, finding seasonal work, accepting Newton Wallace's hospitality and treating him with great respect. In the year that Corey arrived, the gipsies stayed away. And they were never again seen on Manor land. Only she, Newton and the gipsies knew why.

Already, to Corey's eyes, the atmosphere around the Manor had changed. It had an uncomfortable grandeur now it had been partially renovated. She was invited into the huge stone-flagged hall and told to wait. Gloomily, overawed by the richness of the tapestries and highly polished eighteenth-century furniture, she twiddled her bare brown toes in the fringe of a large Persian carpet.

'Good heavens! Tom's little artist friend!'

Corey whirled at the cool tones to see Lydia descending the sweeping stairs.

The contrast between the two women was striking. Dressed in a simple peasant blouse and home-made patchwork skirt that clung tightly to her waist and swirled softly around her tanned legs, Corey felt at a distinct disadvantage. Lydia was wearing a slim, very expensive linen suit in a soft eau-de-Nil colour that emphasised her pale blonde hair.

'I'm not Tom's anything now,' Corey reminded

Lydia fiercely, hating her quiet confidence.

'No.' Lydia paused for effect, one well-manicured hand on the elegantly curving oak banister rail. 'At least you had some sense. What exactly are you doing here?'

'I'm waiting for Mr Radcliffe. We had an appointment at eight.' Corey pointedly glared at the grandfather clock against the wall. Jude was half an hour late already—although, to be fair, she had not long arrived herself.

'If you knew Jude well enough, you'd know to add at least half an hour to any appointment he suggests. He's diabolical. Typical vague, creative type.'

'Creative?' queried Corey. Tom hadn't said anything about that side of him.

'Of course. Don't let the suave exterior fool you. He's a mad artist underneath. The outer casing is all surface veneer. God knows how long you'll have to wait.'

'Damn! I hate hanging around. I've got so much work to do.'

Lydia eyed her speculatively. 'I'm intending to have breakfast. Come and have coffee. We can talk.'

Astonished at the offer and intensely curious about Lydia's intentions, Corey followed the smoothly swaying figure into the breakfast room. To her disappointment, it had not been renovated and was still in the same seedy beige and browns, the wallpaper curling away from one corner where rust-coloured stains marked the path of a burst pipe.

'Terrible taste the old boy had,' complained Lydia. 'Off-putting at breakfast time, to say the least!'

Secretly agreeing, Corey refused to support a stranger against Newton. 'Mr Wallace hardly used more than two rooms,' she said primly. 'He couldn't afford to open up more of the house.'

Lydia snorted inelegantly. 'That's ridiculous. He left Jude stacks of money. Didn't you know? Aren't you curious about the Radcliffe fortune?'

'No. I don't want to know anything about him. It's none of my business.'

'Not curious about Jude? Or afraid of knowing what a yawning gulf lies between you both?'

Corey glared at Lydia's perception. 'All I know is that Mr Wallace never seemed to have much money.'

'No, well, it seems he was a mean old devil. Jude isn't grumbling, though, he can relax his business deals and concentrate on the design side.'

'You know a lot about him.' At Lydia's inviting wave, Corey sat at the damask-covered table and accepted a cup of strong black coffee.

'Darling, I've known him for years. Even, would you believe, *before* he was a committed bachelor.'

'You're trying to tell me something.'

'To warn you. Jude isn't in the market for permanent relationships.'

'Dog in the manger?' murmured Corey in a dangerous voice.

Lydia's eyes gleamed. 'No! He's not susceptible to me. Long ago we settled into a working relationship that has nothing to do with sex. Look, Corey,' she leaned on her elbows with an earnest expression, 'I don't want him to change. The business is doing well and I'm rising with it. Jude devotes all his time to work. Domesticity is death to the artistic temperament. But then you'd know about that.'

'Me?'

'I had a heart-to-heart with him last night. I'm living here while we sort the house out. I'm his chief designer. So,' Lydia selected a bowl of strawberries and poured a tub of natural yoghurt on them. With a speculating look at Corey, she leant back and popped a luscious strawberry into her neat mouth. 'Tread carefully, darling. This time next year you'd be just another memory. He'll have to beat back fortune-hunters now. There'll be plenty of nubile women after him, I can tell you. Looks, power and money make a great trio of aphrodisiac power. There's a long trail of girls, going way back—even in his early days. Not many teenagers get thrown out of boarding school for sleeping with the assistant matron!'

Corey's shocked gasp was drowned by the sound of Jude himself, sweeping into the room. Her heartbeat rose at the sight of his tanned chest, seductively visible in the 'V' of his half-buttoned casual cream shirt, and the tight, faded blue jeans which accentuated danger-ously the muscularity of his long legs.

It was only when he spoke that she raised her eyes to his face and saw how closed his expression was.

'Morning. Sorry I'm late, Corey. Lydia and I were up half the night.'

In silence, he helped himself from the hotplates.

'Perhaps you two would like to have breakfast alone,' suggested Corey pointedly.

'Not particularly. I think Lydia and I sorted out all our problems.'

'How fortunate for you,' commented Corey sarcastically.

Jude raised one eyebrow at Lydia, as though he was giving her a pre-arranged signal.

'I'm going,' said Lydia, wiping her lips delicately. 'Catch up with me in the master bedroom.'

What an exit line! thought Corey in admiration.

'Give me an hour or so,' called Jude. 'I'll attend to Corey, then . . .'

'Then it's my turn,' laughed Lydia, popping her head around the door.

Jude's chuckle followed her out.

'Quite a woman,' he observed.

'You should know.'

Corey poured herself another cup of coffee. She needed time to think. Jude wasn't a business clone after all; he was creative—and rather wild, if Lydia could be believed. Lydia *had* seemed truthful, in fact Corey had almost liked her for her honesty and frankness. But then, perhaps Lydia was very good at hiding her feelings. She might be having an affair with her boss and not wanting anyone else muscling in.

'Has Cat got your tongue?' enquired Jude.

'I'm digesting.'

'Coffee needs digesting?' There was nothing else in front of her but the breakfast cup.

'Information.'

'Ah. Information. Lydia, of course.' He sounded curt. 'Don't believe everything she tells you.'

His attention taken up by ham and eggs, Corey fell silent again, gazing out of the window on to the sloping lawns. She did not know *what* to believe. In the back of her mind was an unpleasant picture that kept thrusting itself forwards: Jude in the arms of a steadily changing queue of women. It was then that she knew he had affected her more than she cared to admit.

An aching surge almost overcame her, nearly propelling her to slip on to his lap and slide her hands inside his crisp shirt and feel the warmth of his skin. Jude's undeniable virility mocked her in the apparently normal and domestic scene. The long table separating them, set in an immaculate perfection of

damask napkins and sparkling silver, thwarted her
hunger for his mobile lips, roaming, exploring,
sensitising. The trap was closing around her—she had
become a prisoner of her own emotional and physical
needs. Her newly won freedom was being threatened.
How ironic. And at breakfast time too! She allowed
herself a small smile, then shot a glance at Jude to see
if he had noticed. No—he was studiously ignoring her,
frowning at his food as though it had bitterly wronged
him.

Corey *had* to do something; she couldn't sit here and
run her eyes over Jude's body much longer. How could
he sit there and not notice the tension she felt! Maybe
Lydia had eased his frustrations last night. She sucked
in her breath and jumped up.

'It's late. I can't afford to hang about watching you
eat,' she said briskly. 'Do we see the gardener or shall I
go home and do some work?'

Jude's face was expressionless. 'I didn't know you
worked to a timetable.'

'I don't. But I dislike being at someone's beck and
call.'

'Everyone has to accommodate other people at
some time,' he observed quietly, studying her.
'However, if you want to get started, the gardener will
be working in the conservatory. Do you know where
that is?'

'Yes. At the back of the house.'

'Tell him I'm just finishing my coffee.'

Walking out of the breakfast room was like
unwinding a rubber band. Both of them were being so
careful, skating around each other, holding back their
real feelings, playing a game of extreme caution.

She ought to keep walking, of course, till she arrived
home. But she hadn't had enough of him. It was like

taking a small bite out of a perfect peach—you had to finish it. But peaches didn't wreak the same havoc that men did.

Taking a short cut, she opened the door to the potting room next to the conservatory. On the benches and work surfaces, where once Mr Wallace and she had planted up seed trays, were now piles of portfolios, and canvases stood stacked up on the floor. Corey's eyes widened. Tentatively she opened a large sketch pad nearest to her.

Mrs Geer in the post office! She was unmistakable—bending anxiously over the ledgers that gave her such angst. Jude had captured exactly the expression of tense determination. Her interest aroused, she flicked quickly through the pages, recognising the village headmaster and Silas, then stopped at the next picture. It was her; an exact image, in her white dress which swirled around naked legs, caught in the act of stamping out a barbaric rhythm, her head held arrogantly high with jutting chin and flashing eyes, surrounded by flying black hair.

Shaken, she took in every detail. It was a drawing of sheer joy. A shiver went down her back at the intense feeling and perception which had gone into every line.

'You weren't supposed to see that,' said Jude, close behind her.

'Oh! I . . . I always look in sketch books if they're left lying around,' she said quickly.

One arm reached past her and swivelled the pad so that he could see the page clearly. His other arm rested lightly on her shoulder.

'Lydia's right. You're very talented,' said Corey.

'Well, it was a labour of love. Though this isn't a patch on the original.'

'You've got a good visual memory,' commented Corey.

'You think so? Could you draw me? Is my image planted firmly in your mind?'

His words rang home. She shut her eyes. Yes, she had absorbed his features into her very being: his moods, his gestures. Every line. Unnerving.

'I thought so,' he smiled, reading her expression.

'Can I see some of your other work?' she asked desperately, moving away and rifling through the portfolios. She extracted a design for a modern house.

'You've made this look grand *and* homely,' she said in admiration.

'That's what most of them want: status symbols which they can live in. I invite myself to their current homes and get the atmosphere. I'm glad you recognised that.'

His hand curled around hers and he raised it to his lips for a feather-light kiss.

Blindly, she turned the pages of a slim pad till her pulse slowed down.

'I don't know why you're a businessman,' she said, pausing in awe at a completed pastel of a child. 'This is so perceptive. Oh, Jude!' This time she had to face him. 'Don't waste yourself! How can you *not* paint and draw every day? Don't you get frustrated at meetings—don't you want to run away and tap your creativity?'

'You understand,' he said slowly, raising his hands to hold her face. 'Yes, I get frustrated.'

'And you rush off?'

'No.' He grinned. 'I stay and get bad-tempered.'

'But . . .'

'Corey. This,' he gestured around the room at the portfolios, 'is my life. You evidently understand how important it all is to me. Yet I have responsibilities that I can't abandon.'

'Let someone else take over,' she urged.

'Not yet. The business needs stabilising.' His eyes gleamed. 'One day I will work how and when I choose.'

She nodded. 'You'll be happy then.'

'Happier. I still would need an empathetic partner.'

I could be that person, thought Corey. If only . . .

'Corey—,' he began.

'I know, Jude,' she said. 'You don't have to say it. We're empathetic up to a point. Trouble is . . .' As she was talking, she had stretched out a hand, flipping through some of the canvases, and before he could stop her, she had paused at an oil painting, studying it intently.

The style was similar to his, but less expert. The canvas showed signs of wear and tear around the edges and had obviously been executed some time ago. Behind her, she felt Jude tense.

'Who is this?' she asked in an unnaturally high voice.

'A woman I knew.'

Corey bit back her next question. No man would spend five minutes in the woman's company without wanting to make love to her. Despite the immaturity of the artist, the woman's raw passion had been captured. But most disturbing was the fact that she had been portrayed as a gipsy dancer, like one of the Gitano women from the caves near Granada. Next to this wild creature, she, Corey, was a pale comparison. She wondered idly whether Jude imagined that in her he had found a reasonable substitute for the woman. That would never be. She wouldn't be compared to anyone, especially this feral woman.

Miserably, Corey laid the canvases back in place.
'We'd better not keep the gardener waiting,' she
said quietly.

'No.' Jude's voice was a mere whisper.

During the discussions with the gardener, Jude
became morose and withdrawn, finally excusing
himself. Relieved at his departure, Corey nevertheless
watched him surreptitiously as he entered the potting
shed and bent to the canvases on the floor. For a long
time he stayed there, looking—she was sure—at the
gipsy woman. Then the gardener drew her to the
Range-Rover for a tour of the lodge houses and she
saw no more.

She had to rush home after making final arrange-
ments with the gardener. It was Midsummer's Day
and only half an hour till noon. Quickly, she snatched
up her basket and removed two garlic bread rolls from
the warming oven, packing them with a cheese and
herb quiche, sweet baby carrots and tiny firm
tomatoes. A thermos of iced tea had already been
made—thank goodness she had planned ahead for
once, not knowing how long she would be at the
Manor.

At the end of the orchard, she laid a gingham cloth
on the sweet grass, spread out the food and leant
against the cracked bark of an old pear tree.

This was one of the rare moments when she wished
she had a watch. There was time to eat first, she was
sure, as long as she kept an eye on the sky.

When the sun seemed nearly overhead, she brushed
away the crumbs and bent forwards over hunched
knees, eyes shut tightly. If she kept wishing for the
next few . . .

Damn! Someone riding in the Manor field. Resolutely she switched her mind back to her wishes.

'Corey? Are you all right?'

Jude. She'd ignore him.

Before she knew it, however, he had dismounted, pushed his way through her broken fence and was kneeling beside her.

'Look, if it's anything I said——' he began.

She *wouldn't* have him break this moment. How dared he invade her privacy? Sneaking a quick look, she saw his shirt sleeves had been rolled up exposing his strong arms—and his watch. Not quite twelve! She had time to get rid of him.

'I'm O.K. Just thinking,' she said. 'I need time on my own.'

He regarded her doubtfully.

''Bye,' she said with a false cheerfulness. If only he would hurry up and leave!

'Why do you keep looking at my watch?' he asked. 'Are you waiting for someone?'

'No. I just . . .' She looked at him speculatively. He cared for her, she was certain. He would give her extra protection at this time. 'Would you do something for me?' she asked slowly.

'Of course.' His voice was gentle.

Corey took another look at his watch. She would trust him. 'Hold my hand and keep still for five minutes.'

'What?'

'Please, you mustn't speak. This is special.'

He looked at her, skirts spread in glorious abandon, black rivers of hair streaming down her back, face uplifted and urgent, full lips parted in anticipation and the slim tanned body whip-firm.

'You're damned right it's special,' he agreed, taking her hand in both of his and gazing into her eyes. There was a faraway look in them.

'Hush,' she said. 'it's almost noon. Midsummer's Day. I need you to watch over me while I wish.'

'What . . .?'

He was silenced with a fierce frown and an impatient squeeze of her slim hand. They sat perfectly still for long, lovely minutes, the sounds of summer drifting around them; the rustling of the leaves in the trees from the light zephyr, small scuttling noises of tiny animals, the faint humming of Corey's bees in the hive at the end of the orchard.

Then, for a short moment, it seemed that all sounds ceased. The whole countryside held its breath. Jude found he was holding his breath too and that his body was tensed. He stared in wonder at the look of fear that was crossing Corey's face. Instinctively, he gripped her hand more tightly in his and leaned forwards to protect her—though from what, he had no idea.

At last she gave a heavy sigh and relaxed. 'All over,' she said, satisfied.

'Do you mind telling me *what* is over?' asked Jude.

'Noon. The dark hour of the day. Noon is always the dark hour, especially today. It's the time when shadows don't exist. Almost anything can happen.'

'If there aren't any shadows, I don't see how it can be a dark hour.'

'It's unnatural. Supernatural.'

'Oh, I see. Can you tell me what you wished for? I'll tell you what I did, if you will.'

'You wished?'

'Of course. I believe in fairies and magic and happy endings.' He smiled. 'I want to believe. I want to think that there's more to us than this conscious world we know. Haven't you ever met someone and felt you knew them at once? That you were immediately on their wave-length and could let down your guard and relax as if you were at home?'

He's talking about us, thought Corey. She raised questioning eyes to his.

'Sweet nightingale, don't fly away from me. Just . . .' He broke off, annoyed at a disturbance in the woods behind them. 'Damn!' he muttered, as two dark-skinned men broke through the undergrowth and approached the orchard gate close by. 'What do they want?'

To Corey's horror, Jude gestured for them to come into the orchard.

'Gipsies,' he explained unnecessarily. 'Doing some work for me. Newton once employed them, apparently. Yes?'

They ignored him, staring at Corey, their coal-black eyes boring into her. Each man stood as still and as steady as a rock, trained since childhood to freeze into total immobility.

Acknowledging them with a nod, Jude frowned at Corey's reaction to the two men. In defensive attitude, she had jumped up and backed until she had been stopped by the fence and now stood with her lower lip trembling and fingers twisting in her patchwork skirt, bare feet digging into the grass as if she wanted to bury them.

'Have you finished the ditching?' called Jude, hoping to get the men on their way and discover what was troubling her.

'That we have, sir.' The man's voice was soft. He ran one finger around the brightly coloured neckerchief but kept his eyes warily on Corey.

'Then I want you to repair those if you can.' Jude pointed to the broken palings of the fence, close to Corey's shrinking body.

'Del! You got nothing else to do instead?'

'I want that done first. Will you do it or not?' Jude was becoming impatient at the inordinate attention the men were giving Corey.

'By God, we will not!'

At the extraordinary vehemence of the man's tone, Jude stared at the gipsies.

'Aye. Anything, Mr Radcliffe. But no jobs on this land.' The other man spat on to the grass between them all.

'And why the devil not?' rasped Jude, rising.

''Tis her.' A work-worn finger pointed at Corey. 'We thought she'd gone when Himself died.'

'Look——' she began, taking a step forward.

'Del!' yelled the men in unison. Together, they turned tail, quite inexplicably, and fled back into the wood, crashing loudly through the bushes.

'What the hell was all that about?' growled Jude. 'Why should great grown men be afraid of you?'

'I'm not telling you! It's none of your business. Don't ever ask me!' shouted Corey, edging towards the house.

'What are you trying to hide? Why don't you trust me?' asked Jude helplessly. 'For heaven's sake, there can never be anything true between us while you refuse to confide in me!'

'I know. I keep trying to make you see that we can't ever be really close. I'm not sharing myself out. Please go away.'

Rage contorted Jude's face. 'Fickle—capricious— all I hate in a woman. And I had the stupidity to think I was falling in love with you!' At her broken sob, he took a step forward, then checked himself. 'If you won't tell me, I'll damn well find out from the gipsies themselves. Maybe then I'll begin to understand you.

Not that it will matter any more!'

Furiously he smashed his way through the broken fence, destroying it further, caught his mare and grabbed the reins. With a vicious kick, he drove his heels hard into the mare's flanks. She reared, unused to such treatment, then recovered and broke into full gallop across the field in the direction of the wood.

Corey watched, holding her breath as the mare took the five-bar gate at the end of the meadow with hardly a check in her stride, and sped straight into the thick of the trees. For a moment there was a crashing, swishing sound of branches and undergrowth, then the noises receded.

'Wow, he's mad,' she muttered. Something evil had happened that noon. She had thought freedom would automatically bring her happiness, but it hadn't. She had wished an end to the complications in her life, and maybe that was what was happening: the arrival of the gipsies might mean exactly that, because Jude would leave her alone once he found out her background. No Lord of the Manor would fancy being seriously entangled with a gipsy girl.

That was just the opposite of what she wanted! She needed a magic wand to make everything all right, for her past never to exist, only the present and future. Being left alone by Jude was the one thing she didn't want. She desired two things: to share herself with Jude, and to have total freedom. Sadly, the two were totally incompatible. And now, the first was certainly impossible.

CHAPTER FOUR

THE school fête was the only village activity that Corey enjoyed. Ever since she had sufficient skill at silversmithing, she had made bangles, ear-rings and brooches suitable to sell, and all the profit she had handed over to the painfully thin, overworked headmaster.

Sedgewood School was nothing like the one where she had spent so many unhappy days. She looked around the thronged playground, bright with banners, streamers, the striped stall awnings and bobbing balloons. Here, the children laughed and chattered, unafraid of adults. The slow learners had a special place in the headmaster's heart—an unheard-of privilege in Corey's school, where they'd stripped and washed her in the cloakroom on that first day, afraid that she would bring some unmentionable diseases into the school. She was cleaner than they were, she thought angrily. But she knew how to submit silently to authority; all gipsies knew how to pay lip-service to bureaucrats.

The humiliation was constant. 'Got any white heather?' the children yelled at her mother, every time she collected Corey. Then, her mother's ragbag of clothes had embarrassed her. Sometimes, despite her hatred and scorn of the *gaje* children, she had wished her mother would dress up when she came to the school. The ridicule was hard to take. Only the ingrained respect for her mother made her stay there, stubbornly silent. But she learnt little, for there was no encouragement, and she knew her mother was disappointed.

Now, extraordinarily, she felt alien to the gipsies. She glanced furtively over to the group on the other side of the netball court. They seemed to be always watching her, their expressions implacable. Any movement that she made away from her stall had them all tensed and waiting.

It was the first year that they'd been at the fair at the same time and it was proving an uncomfortable experience. She was glad to see Tom's friendly face in the crowd.

'How much?' A young girl held up a pair of bobble ear-rings and in doing so, found the tiny price tag.

'Oh, they'll look marvellous on you!' enthused Corey, seeing the girl's crisp, flicked hair-style and puckish face. 'Try them on—here's a mirror.'

Corey smiled at Tom as he approached and was busily packing the ear-rings in tissue when he finally struggled through the crowd and leaned his hands on the stall.

'I wondered where you were, then I saw this dazzling yellow and knew only you would be wearing such a penetrating colour,' grinned Tom.

'It's saffron,' laughed Corey.

'Damned bright in this sun. Anyway, is there any chance of you leaving all this for a moment? Can I whisk you away to ask your advice?' he asked.

'Well . . .' Corey turned to the young boy helping out on the next stall. 'Sam, can you keep an eye on the Crown Jewels for a while? If you're not too busy?'

'Never too busy for you, Miss Lee,' came Sam's slow drawl. 'Don't know about these fripfraps, though.'

'They're all priced. Just sell them,' laughed Corey.

'O.K., will do,' agreed Sam.

'Thanks. Where are we going?' asked Corey. The gipsies had bunched defensively and she didn't want to go past them.

'To have a look at the horses. I'm thinking of buying one. To be honest, I feel jealous of the way friend Radcliffe sits his horse. I fancy myself in boots too.' He smiled down at her. 'Don't you think I'd look rather masterful?'

'Mmmm, very macho. Who said I know anything about horses?'

'I asked Charlie the blacksmith to advise me but he said you were the expert. He reckoned you were a better judge of horse-flesh than him. I must say, you keep your talents well hidden!'

'Not much call for judging horses' qualities,' she said. 'It's something I learnt as a child. Which one are you interested in?'

They had reached the field where six horses were being led around by tough-looking dealers.

'That's what you're here to tell me.'

Corey took her time with her judgment.

'Either of the bays, Tom,' she said finally. 'See which one you take to.'

She stood close to him, as she showed him how to talk to each one, smoothing slow, mesmeric hands over their cushioned noses and making snuffling noises at them.

Tom bent his head down to her. 'Sounds like you've got an acute touch of asthma,' he murmured.

As Tom spoke in what to an outsider must have seemed an intimate way, and as Corey's tinkle of laughter sparked her eyes, Jude chose to walk by with Lydia. The distress he felt was clear for Lydia to see and she gasped as his courteous grip on her arm tightened painfully.

Mindlessly, and taking no notice of Lydia's protest, he bundled her unceremoniously into the nearest tent. Anything to escape the sight of Corey and Tom so cosily affectionate. Had their affair revived?

'Welcome. Which one first?'

They both started at the voice coming from the gloom, their eyes not accustomed to the dim light after the brightness of the sun outside.

'If the lady would sit down?' said the voice again.

Their eyes focused on a weather-worn face, dominated by black all-seeing eyes and a strong nose.

'My name is Tshaya,' she said in her soft voice. 'Don't be afraid. Put out your hands, lady.'

Obediently, Lydia sat down and stretched out her hands, which were immediately gripped. Jude hovered in the back- ground while the woman reeled off rapidly a surprisingly accurate character sketch, and promised the satisfied Lydia great success in the future.

'Now you, sir,' said the woman, staring hard at him.

'I want some information first,' he said, keeping his hands in his lap.

She frowned. 'Information's extra.'

'Fine. I'll pay. You're one of the gipsies who are by the ford, on my land?'

'Aye. You're Newton Wallace's boy, then.' Her gimlet eyes softened.

'His nephew. Two of your men refused to work on land where one of my tenants lives. Why?'

Lydia was looking at him curiously. The woman leaned back and sucked in her breath.

'That Corey Lee. She be *marimé*—outcast. She could make us *marimé* too if we touch her. Then we has to travel apart from the rest. None of us wants that.'

Jude leaned forwards. 'Just what do you mean? What has she ever done to you?'

'Ask her. She must decide if you are to know. You're a *gaje*, a non-gipsy. God blind me two eyes if I tell a *gaje* any gipsy business. But give me your hand a minute.'

Frowning, his mind on Corey, and wondering what she had done to offend these people so deeply, he absently placed his hands on the table.

'Two men come between you and what you want. Your woman leaves you soon and goes to one of them. She has . . .'

'I don't want to hear any more!' cried Jude, standing abruptly. Nonsense or not, he was in no mood to hear this woman saying what he feared. 'Here, take this.' He thrust money into her hand.

'Is . . . is Corey in danger?' he asked, unable to prevent himself from half-believing in the gipsy's powers.

'I reckons she is.'

'By God!' he snarled, suddenly animal-like in his fury. 'If any of you hurt her, I'll burn down your bloody camp!'

'The danger is from you. And you talk of fire: there is fire, but not in our camp. And you will part in sorrow.'

The woman's eyes bored into his skull, burning a message. Jude gave a half-scornful laugh, trying to shake off the dramatic effect of her words.

'There's more,' she said.

Jude refused to hear more. 'Let's get out of this place,' he muttered.

Blindly he wandered around the fête, allowing the worried Lydia to steer him. For appearance's sake,

Jude had to stay a while, visiting each stall. He spotted the two men who had run away from Corey, mending broken saucepans and sharpening knives, but they took no notice of him. To his relief, Corey had packed up and gone—probably with Tom, entertaining him in her cosy little cottage. Or her cosy little bedroom. He kicked at a wall.

'I've never known you so moody,' said Lydia anxiously. 'She's really got under your skin, hasn't she?'

'Yes.' He rubbed his lip. 'I'm getting a taste of my own medicine. I could never understand why women got so involved with me when I didn't care for them. Now I know it's possible to feel very deeply for someone, even if they only have superficial feelings for you.'

'It's more than a passing passion, then?'

'I don't know! I'm trying to kid myself that's all it is. I emphatically don't want to get mixed up with her. I'm sorry for shouting at you, Lydia. I'm bad company. Let me go and ride the hell out of Moonlight. I'll be vaguely civilised for dinner then. Take the car, I'll walk back over the fields.'

Corey had enjoyed her afternoon. The goods on her stall had been sold out early, so she had bought one or two items—keeping a healthy distance between herself and the wary gipsies—and wandered slowly home, leaving Tom to arrange for his newly-acquired horse to be stabled locally.

The summer evening beckoned after supper, and Corey strolled to the brook, sitting on the mossy bank and bending forwards to search for tiddlers. She had a considerable shock, when a pair of berry brown hands descended on her shoulders. There had been no sound and her hearing was acute. She sat rigidly, waiting for something awful to happen.

'That's a real nice dress, *na*,' said a man's voice.

'Salf!' she swung around, under his hands, jumped up and flung herself into his arms. 'Oh, Salf, it's been so long! Why don't you come more often?' she scolded.

Her brother grinned and pulled her down to the bank, loosening the bright red cotton scarf around his neck. She caught hold of his hands, scarred and bruised from accidents with chisels over the years, calloused and hard from sheer grinding hard work.

'You knows us. We goes where the wind takes us.'

Salf always arrived silently from the woods and swept her off on his horse to his camp site miles away, usually near a town, where there was a better market for their work.

He examined her critically. 'You be thin. I remembers when you was as round as a little pig.'

'That was puppy fat. And I only look thin next to you.' Corey spread her hands over his huge chest. With his shirt-sleeves rolled up to his biceps, he looked more like a prize wrestler than the skilled artist that he was. 'Is Ma here? Is she staying?' She sounded wistful.

'No. She won't stay while the Rom is in Wallace's meadow. They go soon, then she'll come. That's why I'm here. You must know the new man in the Manor. Ask if Ma can camp in your orchard. We has to talk with you.'

'Oh, I can't!' This would be the first time her mother had visited here. She couldn't go to Jude and ask if her gipsy relatives could stay for a while on his land!

'You don't want us?' Persalf's face was puzzled.

'Oh, yes, but . . .'

'Listen, sister. Long ago we know you were the

clever one. Ma tried to get you a *gaje* education and you done well. But don't you forget who you are, not ever. There's nothing bad about being a Rom. It makes me proud.'

'It's easier for you. I'm neither one thing nor the other. Our family has been cast out by the gipsies so I can't join them. I was brought up in both cultures and ended up in neither. I'm alien to both. Who am I? When I'm with the *gaje* I feel like a gipsy. When I see you, I know I'm not. Yet being a gipsy is in my blood, Persalf. I've tried to make a life for myself and to settle down, but I don't think I have it in me.' She was so miserable suddenly, knowing how badly she fitted into both worlds, feeling rootless. She began to sob.

Persalf's muscular arms grasped her tightly and, safe with the only man she could completely trust, she let all the muddled emotions of the last few days flow out with her tears. He rocked her like a baby, crooning in the Romany language. He knew that there must be a man involved in her distress and was prepared to wait patiently until she was ready to unburden herself.

Jude had ridden Moonlight far across country, endangering both their lives in his headlong gallop. At last, wearied and with his problems unsolved, he slowed the mare to a walk and turned her head for home.

A stray horse was grazing by the edge of his wood: a glossy black stallion. Unless someone had made a recent purchase, it belonged to no one that he knew. As he drew near, he saw that it had no saddle, nor any reins. It must have escaped. He was envious of its beautifully powerful lines, from its proud, tossing head to its thick, trailing tail. Whoever owned this massive black beast certainly looked after it well; it was in the peak of condition. And what a horseman you would have to be to ride it! The stallion's ears pricked in his direction and Jude admired the wary intelligence in the proud head that tossed a warning.

He dismounted. Although it was a little nervous, the stallion allowed him to stroke its flanks, but when he tried to catch hold of the gleaming mane, it backed away, into the wood. Jude followed, hoping to trap it somehow. It was then that he became aware of the crying.

The stallion halted, his ears pricked up. Jude stood between the two horses uncertainly, then tiptoed closer. A dark-skinned gipsy was sitting with his broad back to him, apparently caressing a gipsy girl. Jude smiled and turned to leave them in privacy, thinking for a moment that there had been some lovers' tiff, for the man was bending his black curls tenderly to the girl, murmuring soft, foreign-sounding words of consolation and love. But as he turned, out of the corner of his eye he saw a flash of brilliant yellow and he knew, he knew instantly that he had surprised Corey in some woodland assignation.

'My God!' he breathed.

The man whirled around rapidly, springing to his feet, the light glinting on a small knife in his left hand. Jude heard Corey's gasp of horror and his mouth twisted into a sneer. She placed her slender brown hand on the gipsy's massive fist and the knife was returned to the leather sheath on his belt.

The dark form of the stallion pushed Jude to one side as it trotted up to the gipsy and nuzzled him affectionately. Not only had the man won Corey's affection, he was also the owner of that magnificent stallion! Jude felt like a thwarted child in his envy and petulance.

'You're both trespassing,' said Jude coldly.

'You said I could go on your land, whenever and wherever I liked,' said Corey, her tears drying on her cheeks. Jude thought he'd never seen her so vulnerable, so desirable. Her mouth was parted, her eyes misty and soft. The gipsy put his free arm around her and tucked her into him protectively. A lancing heat of jealousy ran through Jude like quicksilver. The man was huge but he wanted to fight him. It was a fierce, primal instinct, irrational and foolish. He'd be beaten to a pulp.

'That didn't include your gipsy lovers,' he said tightly, resenting the man's virility.

'This your land?' asked the gipsy, unaffected by his tone and not bothering to correct him. He was used to aggression and took no notice.

'You're damn right it is. Get off it at once!'

'Ask him,' whispered Persalf to Corey. ''Tis him, isn't it?'

She took one look at Jude's merciless face. He must know that she was a gipsy, that was why he imagined Persalf was her lover. He might as well think that, she supposed. How scornful he looked! 'I can't, I can't ask him,' she muttered.

'Then I will.' Persalf stepped forwards, and stood submissively, his dark-smudged eyes lowered. Corey knew he was assuming a role of humility so that Jude would be mollified. 'Sir, me and my Ma wants to stay for a bit with Corey. We got a wagon. You let us camp in the orchard over there?' He waved an arm towards Corey's garden.

'Why not?' said Jude bitterly. 'Better still, why not live in her cottage?'

'Don't like houses' grinned Persalf. 'Thanks, mister. Corey, I got to go now or I won't be back before dark. We found a halt just this side of Granford. They threatened to move us, so we only got a bit longer there. We'll be along soon. Got things to tell, good things, cheer you up, they will.'

Knowing that Persalf would never travel after dark, she put on a brave face for him.

'Yes, I know you ought to leave. I'm O.K. now. Goodbye, my Rom. Take care.'

She lifted her face and he kissed her, Rom-fashion, full on the lips, holding her shoulders and gazing fondly at her for a moment.

'I'll be back before the new moon, *an* the dear God is willing.'

'I need you. Come quickly. I need you both,' she cried. She'd burnt her boats. Faced with the caring strength of her brother, she didn't care how shocked the village was at the revelation of her parentage, nor what anyone thought about her family—she wanted Persalf near at this time. He'd always protected her in the days when she'd come home from school, either in a rage or in tears. In his arms she reverted to her old role. For too long she'd stood on her feet and battled her way through life on her own. It was wonderful to have such comfort and uncritical support again. Corey buried her face deep in his magnificent chest.

'May my blood spill if I don't make you happier soon,' he muttered.

Jude turned away helplessly, attempting to gather the remnants of control, shattered by the effect this scene was having on him. This man possessed her! A vortex whirled inside him like the centre of a storm; a hurricane, threatening to swell into violent action.

Persalf and Corey were too wrapped up in each

other to notice. Salf cared nothing for the vagaries of the *gaje*. They were always acting oddly. He gently extricated himself from Corey's clinging arms and she lifted her face trustingly. His soft black eyes were moist. Like most gipsies, he was highly emotional. He snatched away his hands, rubbing his huge fists hard into his eyes and reached up to the stallion, vaulting easily on to its back. The horse skittered, full of spirit, but Persalf's strong thighs and gentle hands settled him and he grasped its flowing mane with one hand, bending to chuck Corey under the chin with the other. With a brief nod to Jude, he walked the horse slowly out of the wood, ducking lithely under overhanging branches.

Corey watched him leave, then glanced in an embarrassed way at Jude and averted her gaze immediately in stunned surprise. Every muscle in his face and body was clenched. His teeth were bared, his eyes flickering dangerously, following Persalf's distant figure. Then he turned the penetrating gaze to her.

'He loves you.'

'Yes,' she answered truthfully.

'You love him?'

'Deeply.'

'My God,' he breathed, 'you're quite amoral! Don't you have any idea of propriety?'

'Jude, he . . .'

'I don't want to hear your excuses,' he snarled. 'You're like a bitch on heat with all the dogs in the neighbourhood sniffing around you!'

'That's disgusting!' she cried.

'Yes, it is! I don't know how you do it, Corey, but you seem to draw men from tycoons down to gipsies.'

'*Down* to gipsies?' she said in a warning tone.

Yes—down. You can't get more basic than that raggle-taggle Romany lover. And you had the temerity to deny *me*!' His pride was incalculably wounded, and his opinion of Corey had taken a bad knock. He knew she was unconventional, but this . . .

'You snob!' she cried, amazed.

'No, I'm not! Hell, Corey I've no idea what I'm saying. I want you. For years I've been aware of the woman I want and now you're here and damn well available to every blasted man, it seems, except me. I mean to have you, Corey.' His eyes blazed feverishly.

'Not by indulging such unsubtle, bullying behaviour, you won't,' she retorted.

'You mean the gipsy is subtle?' asked Jude derisively.

'I'm not listening to any more of this,' snapped Corey. 'You're behaving abominably!'

She half turned, watching him warily, but was not quick enough to stop him snaking out an arm and spinning her around again.

'You *will* listen. We'll settle things now.'

'There's nothing to settle,' she said wearily, hating the bitterness. 'What I do and who I befriend is nothing to do with you. My life is my own and I intend to keep it that way. You have no place in it, Jude Radcliffe.'

'So women like you do run true to type,' he grated savagely.

'What are you talking about?'

'I knew a woman like you once. Just like you. She broke as many hearts as bedsprings.'

'Serves the men right,' said Corey without thinking, only wanting to hurt him in return.

'You heartless bitch!'

She thought then he would strike her. An instinct

told her to run: he was close to a mental and physical explosion. Her feet flew over the ground, but he was running after her, crashing heavily through the wood. She increased her pace. His long legs covered the ground far faster than hers; already she could hear his laboured breathing more loudly and a string of continuous curses.

In the garden, close to the house, he caught her up and with a rough, contemptuous movement, pushed her hard against the sun-warmed wall. The impact stunned the breath from her.

'Crunch time,' he said hoarsely.

'Not while you're in this mood, please!'

His hand reached for her chin in a bruising grip.

'You're mine! *Mine!*' he growled.

'No! I'm *mine!*'

But the words were drowned in his mouth which covered and mastered her lips.

The veneer of civilisation had been stripped away. She was terrified. In a desperate attempt to free herself and get some sense into him, she wriggled like an eel, almost slipping from his grasp, but just in time he captured her again, his fingers pressing deep into the flesh of her arms.

In retaliation, her sharp white teeth bit into his lower lip and drew blood. For a moment he snapped back his head, shocked.

'Jude!' she gasped. 'Are you mad? You're hurting me! Stop it!'

'Mad? Yes, I am,' he rasped. 'Raving, ranting mad. And it's your fault. You've driven me mad! I never knew just what you were till just now. Free? My God, you're free! Particularly with your body!'

'That's not true . . .' she started.

'Don't lie to me!' he shouted. 'First my uncle gets

into your bed, then Tom, and now I find you're available to any gipsies who happen to wander by. And that's only the men I know about, God knows how many others there are. Is that why those gipsies were afraid of you? That they'd be enchanted like the rest of us? I swear to you, if you're going to entertain a gipsy lover on *my* grass by *my* river under *my* trees, then by God you'll also have me. And if you like your men rough, like that barbaric gorilla, then I can be that, too. You've had this coming a long time. Ever since I first met you, you've been working me slowly up to this. You're more subtle and wily than any woman who's tried to land me. Well done! Congratulations!'

'I *haven't* planned this! I hate violence! I don't like being hurt!' she cried.

'I know the answer now.' His feverish eyes burned molten grey into hers. 'Not to listen, just act. You want natural reactions, you're going to get them.'

At that, he ground his body full into hers. The crudity of the gesture and his highly aroused state both shocked and stunned her. He was going to . . .

'Jude! You're frightening me!'

'You're frightened? I'm terrified, Corey. You're tearing apart everything I've built up over the years— my self-control, a rational, considered approach to life and a conscious decision not to let any woman dominate my emotions. I wouldn't mind so much if you had one ounce of morality in your body—if I thought you'd play fair. But you flirt and lead me on, and make me believe you care, when all you want is pure unadulterated gratification. So that's what you're going to get.'

'You think so little of me?' she said quietly.

'What else can I think? That's what you show me every time.'

With a quick gesture, she wrenched from his grasp and ducked under his arms but he caught her quite effortlessly. In fury born of a pain, caused by his humiliatingly low opinion, she wrestled with him silently, giving no quarter, using her teeth, nails, elbows, knees and feet to inflict as much damage as she could. His defence was to pin her against the wall with his body and amid the violence she felt a hot stirring flame rising and filling her whole body. Her eyes kindled.

'Damn you, Corey,' he groaned.

His mouth descended to capture hers and his hands tightened around her arms, making her moan in pain. Releasing his grip immediately, Jude saw dark imprints where his fingers had bruised the skin. Miserably, he ran a hand through his hair.

'I'm sorry! I had no idea I was hurting you.'

She didn't answer. He turned his back, despair showing in his clenching fists and bowed head.

'Oh hell! I just want to say——' She could hardly hear the muttered words and moved closer, aware of the maelstrom of his mind, and hers '—I've found it impossible to handle the emotions you've aroused. They're too damn bitter-sweet. Too violent and tender. I love you, Corey.'

With that, he faced her and she caught her breath at his pain-racked face and moist eyes. Her own eyes filled with tears for them both.

'Forgive me,' he continued blindly. 'I know I've ruined everything now, but please understand. By God, I'd defy a saint to check the passions I feel!'

For a long moment, their eyes locked, hot grey and

melting brown. And she recognised fully the depth of his feelings.

'I'm ensnared, utterly enslaved,' he said.

'You don't like that?'

'Would you?'

'No. Yes. Well, I hate the idea of having my identity swallowed up by someone.'

'I know.' There was a distant look of pain in his eyes, as though he was elsewhere. 'I was hurt by a woman who loved freedom.'

'I see.'

Jude frowned at the softened lines of her face and a wary look crept into his expression.

'Don't be nice to me. Don't offer sympathy,' he said. 'I couldn't bear it.'

His vulnerability tore at her tender heart and she reached up a gentle hand to brush away the moisture at the corners of his eyes. A man who could feel so deeply wouldn't hurt her, surely. He'd treat her feelings with respect.

Locked in the fierce morality of the Rom, Corey had previously held her passions in check. Something had always stopped her from allowing her body to rule her head. This time, everything was right. Jude of all men had the power to touch her soul. An intense longing, more than merely a physical need, shook her body. She felt that without him she was only half-made.

She only had a second or two to make her decision before he drew so far away that the moment would be lost.

'I trust you. Trust me,' she said gently.

'I wish I could.'

'Maybe this will help.' Her honey voice melted his resolve. Corey kissed him lightly on the cheek. 'Stop these attacks on me. I always fight back, it's instinctive. I prefer seduction.'

He said nothing but she knew by the tension in his body what conflicts raged within. She must take the lead and commit herself by giving him everything. Only then might they both dare to let the relationship grow.

'How will we know what we mean to each other unless we take the next step?' she murmured.

With a gentle tug at the shoe-string straps of her yellow dress, she allowed the dress to slide down her body. Jude closed his eyes to her nakedness, his breathing heavy and ragged.

'Don't torment me like this,' he rasped.

She leaned back against the wall. How much more control did he have? Impulsively, she snapped off the stem of a wild white rose close by.

'Listen to your heart, Jude. All the truths are in there.'

Between her slender fingers, the rose swept lightly across her lips as Jude watched fascinated, through hooded eyes. Corey's own desire was surging powerfully to an all-consuming heat. The rose slowly circled her breasts and drifted lightly, backwards and forwards across the swelling nipples. As she fixed Jude with her eyes and he began to remove his jacket blindly, the rosy centres of her breasts tightened and lengthened, knowing what was to come.

Very, very languidly, he unbuttoned his shirt and very, very slowly, Corey traced the lines of her body until the rose lay snowy white against the dark triangle of hair.

'I don't understand,' he muttered. 'Could any man understand you?'

Her tantalising eyes slanted at him, his pulse quickened and he reached out to duplicate with his fingers the same path taken by the rose. Her eyes closed of their own volition, heavy and languorous, and she stood immobile, savouring the delicacy of his touch. And then his lips took up the trail and they sank to the ground as Corey began to move her body like a wanton, scorching Jude's skin with her own fevered kisses, the slow tender exploration abandoned in a rising tide of desire.

'Wait, Corey.' His voice cracked with passion. 'This will be very special for me. Don't push me beyond endurance. I want this to last.'

The tenderness of his lovemaking shook her. All the while, he talked to her, exclaiming over her body as he touched it, telling her what he was going to do, telling her how she made him feel, and what pleasure she gave him. The verbal assault was even more potent than any blatantly sexual one. It shattered her senses and pulled on her emotions. Relentlessly he talked, sometimes hoarsely, sometimes so quietly that she could barely hear the words. But he seduced her utterly with his voice and with loving phrases, tormenting her with his total control until her mind and body became fused with his and she clung to his firm, gold-smooth body, picking up his rhythm as its insistence pounded into her senses and the whole of her existence seemed focused on the union of her movements and Jude's silver voice, murmuring in her ear.

Her head rocked from side to side. Wave upon wave of shuddering fire leapt through her body. One final surge drew from her a wild cry of release and she called Jude's name over and over again. There was no pain as she had expected, only complete satiation of all her senses. Above her, Jude gasped her name and he finally relaxed, burying his face in her neck.

They lay together, stroking each other gently in the

aftermath of their passion, sliding quietly into sleep. Jude's arms protected Corey and the last thing she remembered was the trickling of fire in her veins and total peace.

They slept moulded together until they both woke, chilled in the night air. Wordlessly, unwilling to break the spell, they helped each other up and stumbled into the cottage, climbing into Corey's bed.

She woke after Jude. They were squashed together rather uncomfortably and he had raised himself on one elbow to study her.

She blushed under his scrutiny, finding their intimacy suddenly shocking in the daylight. Last night it had all seemed inevitable, so right. Now she realised what a huge difference there was in sleeping with a man. She was completely vulnerable, dangerously exposed by his possession.

Jude tipped up her chin and she was unable to avoid his eyes.

'Don't,' she said, wanting to hide.

'Regrets?'

She searched his face of signs of triumph, or capture, or maybe an air of ownership. He smiled down at her, innocent of all these, blissful happiness emanating from every pore.

'No,' she breathed, closing her eyes in relief.

'Your eyelashes are like bat's wings when you're asleep,' he said in wonder.

She smiled. 'That's a compliment?'

'Yes. In my eyes, you are perfect. That's a compliment, if you hadn't recognised it.'

'Mmmm. I feel I never want to get up. That's not being perfect, that's lazy.'

'It's not surprising, though. Let's stay in bed all day.'

'What! And miss adding to the Radcliffe millions? How irresponsible can you get?'

'Very,' he answered cryptically. 'That's what I'm afraid of. Too many people rely on me now.'

Corey smiled. 'When I remember what I first thought of you, all suave and public-schooly . . . What would your fellow tycoons say, if they'd seen you last night?' The idea amused her enormously.

'After all that's happened, you seem very much at ease.'

'Shouldn't I be?' she asked, puzzled. They had made glorious perfect love and she was content. What could be better?

'Happens to you often does it?' Jude's face looked thunderous.

'No, damn you. Why spoil it by saying that?'

He swung out of the bed and stood, naked, at the window. She caught her breath to see his hard, healthy body.

'I can't get the other men out of my mind.' He ran his fingers through unruly brown waves. 'I know it's stupid, I know it's chauvinistic, that your body is your own and you can do what you like with it, but I can't cope with the idea that you're so free.'

'I see. After all that, you still don't trust me.' A stab of disappointment ran through her. 'I suppose it's fine that *you* can be free?' She was damned if she was going to admit that Tom was only her friend and that Salf was *not* her lover! And as for old Mr Wallace! Besides, Jude had women, lots of them. She wasn't *very* jealous, why should he be? 'You've made love to dozens of women. I don't go around sulking because of them.'

'There haven't been that many,' he said distractedly.

'What about the assistant matron?'

'Who? Good lord, I only kissed her.'

'I heard different. I heard you'd been thrown out of school because you'd made love to her.'

'That was a rumour among the boys—which I did nothing to deny because it made me feel great. And it didn't harm her because she was leaving that term to work as a nanny abroad. I was actually asked to leave because of my eccentric habits. They didn't like me getting up in the middle of the night to paint, or dreaming in lessons, or occasionally leaving them when an idea struck me. They weren't madly keen to discover me painting nudes, either. I was considered a bad influence, recalcitrant, obstinate and unmalleable. I broke too many rules.'

'Oh.'

The bed depressed as Jude sat down beside her.

'Look,' he said, taking her hand, 'this isn't getting us very far. I can't stand the way we're living at the moment. I love you, Corey. I want you with me, not flitting about enticing half the gipsies in the neighbourhood. You're very young and naïve. That—that man in the wood. He seemed as if he cared for you, much as I hate to admit it. You were obviously not a one-night stand for him. But it was a dangerous thing to do. They're strange people, these gipsies. They've got different morals and different ways from us. You shouldn't let yourself get mixed up with them.'

Corey stared at him. So he really didn't know. He hadn't managed to prise her secret from those men. What was she to do now?

'Marry me,' continued Jude. 'Let's put a stop to all this madness. If I have to carry on like we are at the moment, I'll be bankrupt within the year.'

'Is that what you care about?' asked Corey quietly.

'No! It's my sanity I care about. I'm going crazy.'

He touched the dark bruises on her arms and bent to kiss them sweetly. 'I'll never forgive myself for attacking you, even if you do,' he said thickly. 'I want you to come and live with me as my wife. I never thought I'd say that to any woman. If you like, we'll stay in the Manor and I'll commute to London like Tom. I can't see you liking London much. Well, will you?'

A familiar fear stabbed into Corey's heart, She clutched at the sheet that covered her.

'No, Jude, I can't marry you. Already you want me to give up my home. I love it. I wouldn't be comfortable in that big house nowadays.'

'I'll tear half of it down!' he suggested wildly, a glint of humour in his eyes.

'It's not only that. You want to stop me roaming around . . .'

The humour receded abruptly. 'Of course!' he stormed. 'You're too provocative! Any man has only to look at your wicked sexuality and you'd be fair game.'

'There goes your trust again,' she said in a low voice.

'Oh hell.' He covered his face with his hands. 'I don't know what to think, what to say. Rationality seems to have left me. I don't know how to handle this. Corey, I want marriage. I want you more than anything in the world and my jealousy tempts me to lock you away for my eyes only. But I'm afraid of trapping you, I know it would take the life from you. I want my nightingale to sing. Yet is it any wonder I don't want my nightingale singing for someone else?'

She sat up moodily and hugged her knees. '*Your* nightingale? I can't be yours. I can share my body with you,' she ran a trembling finger down his thigh and he gasped, 'but that's all. Jude, I'm not promiscuous. I expect you to believe me. And if you don't then I can't see our relationship building on anything stable. Shall I tell you what I'd like? For us to live where we do: you at the Manor and me here and for you to make love to me sometimes.'

'It's not enough,' he said hoarsely.

'Then you must find a wife elsewhere,' she said tremulously, hating the idea. 'I'm not marrying you. You see, when I was a child, I was illiterate and very poor. I came from a single-parent family. My schooldays were spent in utter humiliation. I've fought and struggled to find a place in this world where I can be proud of what I do. Newton Wallace helped me to gain enough confidence to cope with the life I have, but I can't go further up the social scale—I tried it with Tom and it was a dismal failure. When I meet assured people, especially those from your walk of life, I shrink back to being insecure and unhappy. You and your friends have all the poise of knowing that you've been well educated, schooled in how to behave in every imaginable situation. You have an inborn ability to wield personal authority with charm and panache. I'm not in your league. I'm not prepared to aspire to it.'

'You're being ridiculous!' he began.

'I'm not! You saw for yourself how I stuck out like a sore thumb at that dinner with Tom's parents. It was a fiasco. I've nothing in common with people like that.'

Jude clicked his tongue impatiently. 'For heaven's sake, Corey, don't judge everyone by them. Lettice Gowrie-Dyson is a bit of a stickler for upper-crust etiquette, but my friends aren't like that. They're all mad Bohemian types, as bad as you,' he said with a twisted smile. 'You've got a massive—and very unneccessary—inferiority complex.'

'You'll be telling me how you'd teach me how to socialise and act as your hostess next,' Corey accused sharply.

'Of course I won't!' he said irritably. 'Try meeting my friends, you'll be surprised. People don't care about that sort of thing any more, they'd be much more interested in *you*.'

Me? thought Corey. Yes, they'd be fascinated. My dear, you're the daughter of a gipsy? Does she sell clothes-pegs? She shuddered.

'You *are* being irrational. You're not seeing how disastrous it would be. For both our sakes, I won't marry you,' she said stubbornly.

Jude gave an exasperated sigh. 'All right, have it your own way—for the moment. I'll saunter back to my grand manorial home, have a breakfast of oysters and Buck's Fizz off gold plate, get the butler to polish my shoes and then I'll take the Porsche to the Design Centre in London where I'll sit all day sipping champagne and eating caviare.'

'You're being silly!'

'No, you are,' he said shortly. 'I'm just a normal man in love. Uncontrollably in love. I intend to pester you till you relent. I mean to have you for my wife. You can count on that. And let me tell you, my determination has won over far harder cases than you.'

Barely controlling his distress, he rose and walked naked down the stairs. Corey heard the door slam. By lying very still, she could just make out the sounds as he found his discarded clothes. Her gate creaked. He had gone.

A long sigh escaped from her lips. The glowing aftermath of Jude's lovemaking had brought on a delicious lassitude. But in her mind a tempest raged. Class barriers didn't seem to make any difference to him, he still wanted to marry her. Foolish man. And apparently a few imaginary lovers didn't matter to him either—they enraged him, but they didn't detract from her eligibility.

Maybe she should relate the whole of her origins to him. It was really no surprise that the gipsies hadn't talked to Jude. It was their habit to keep themselves something of a mystery, filling everyone's heads with half-truths and pure fiction.

She touched her tender breasts in memory of his lovemaking. Her hip-bones ached from the thrusting contact of his body. Passion worthy of a gipsy! Now if she *did* marry Jude and they had a son, how would he cope if he was as dark as Persalf? Would his parents mind? Corey frowned. Jude had never even mentioned parents. But even if he had none, his friends would be horrified. It was an impossible match and he must surely see that.

Cat entered the window, having scrambled along an overhanging branch of the apple tree. Greeting him affectionately, she noticed from the smell of him that he'd been ratting in the barn again.

'You're the only male I'll let in my bed for a long time,' she muttered into his warm back, snuggling into the bedclothes. 'You and Salf are the only two who'll live alongside me. All the others want to stake claims. I feel like a bit of real estate.'

She thought fondly of Persalf and her mother. The sun's rays patterned the floor and martins chattered above her window. Cat pricked up his ears and uttered a low growl. He leaped from her grasp and was out of the window before she could stop him.

'Cat!' she shouted ineffectively, stumbling on shaky legs. He'd been after those martins ever since they started building the nest. Now, with the young

fledglings taking early flying lessons, they were in
danger of ending up in Cat's stomach. 'You come back
here!'

A sudden flurry caught her eye. On the fringe of the
wood, a handful of starlings rose, like a scattering of
grain. They soared into the sky, dispersing rapidly.
Somewhere a sparrow-hawk must be hovering. Then
she saw it, the unmistakable shape of its blunt wings
and circling glide, then the downward plunge with
folded wings, taking it with incredible speed and
power to its victim. With a chilling finality, the hawk
grabbed its prey and within seconds one more starling
was dead, overwhelmed by an alien of its own kind
more powerful and dominant.

It was then that Corey came to a decision. She
wouldn't let Jude overwhelm her with his power. Let
him find someone from his own set. Nothing in her
past had fitted her for acting Lady of the Manor.

Leaving Cat and the martins to Fate, she tumbled
down the stairs two at a time and pumped up some ice-
cold water into the white sink. The faint odour of
Jude's body clung to her. It took a lot of scrubbing to
smell like herself again.

She threw some clothes into a small bag, shut up the
house and collected the eggs, throwing out a generous
amount of grain on to the orchard grass. Thank
heavens the hens could fend for themselves. Cat, if he
didn't manage a lunch of house martins, was never in
danger of starving if she left him for a few days. His
distended belly this morning was evidence of that.

The road to Granford lay east. She drove towards
the blinding sun, relieved beyond measure to be
leaving. In an hour she would be there, pouring out her
heart to Salf and Ma.

CHAPTER FIVE

PARKED in a country lay-by, a couple of miles outside
Granford, was an ancient ex-Post Office van, painted
in violent primary colours, together with an ornate
new caravan. Slowing the car, Corey recognised Salf's
horse, tethered by a peg to the grass verge.

Outside sat her mother; small, dark-skinned and
with piercing jet-black eyes. Her dark curly hair was
covered with a bright blue scarf, knotted at the nape of
the neck.

'Welcome, daughter,' said Rupa Lee, hardly looking up from her work.

Was her mother never surprised to see her? Corey
bent low over the tiny figure, holding her tightly, and
the strong brown arms wrapped around her in a
squeezing hug, then released their hold suddenly.
Rupa busied herself with unnecessarily smoothing the
silk which lay on her lap.

Corey sat on the ground, close to her mother's full
skirts, leaning against her and breathing in the scent
of fresh lavender that emanated from their multi-
coloured folds. The black beetle eyes rested on her
speculatively and one work-worn hand gently stroked
her hair—a rare gesture, for her mother was extremely
undemonstrative.

'Kettle's still hot in the wagon. Coffee's in the jug.
Go quiet, Persalf's sleeping.'

Obediently Corey tip-toed into the caravan and
brought out the coffee. She relaxed in a deckchair
beside her mother, drinking quantities of the fierce

black coffee that drew at her throat. Times *had* changed. Before this chrome-covered caravan there had been a rusty old van in which they had lived. Before that, she remembered a wooden vardo, the typical wagon of the fairy tales. She'd loved it.

Pity she wasn't living in a fairy tale now. A magic wand might help a lot. 'Ma, I've got to talk to you,' she said, swirling the dark coffee around the mug.

'Yes.' Rupa Lee's bright eyes watched her daughter's nervous fingers.

'Why I'm here.'

'You need a reason to see me?' asked Rupa.

'No, but there is one.'

Rupa cut expertly into the poppy-coloured silk on her knee. 'A man.'

Corey sighed. 'A man,' she agreed.

'The one you're promised to?'

'No, not Tom. I've broken off the engagement. We weren't right for each other.'

'Persalf spoke of an angry man—the one at the Manor. He the one? He loves you?'

'Oh! No . . . Well, he says he loves me, but I don't think it's that. I have a feeling that he wants to capture me—that I'm something of a challenge. He's like a hunter who can't give up on his prey. Oh, Ma, I'm afraid of being tied down!'

'He'd do that?'

'He's very possessive. I think his jealousy could become unmanageable. If he loved me, surely he'd be more trusting?.'

Silk petals fell into heaps on Rupa's lap. She concentrated on pinning them together before she answered. 'Listen, my baby, I reckons you're too young to know about love.'

'Young! I'm twenty-two!'

'Huh!' scorned her mother. 'A bit of paper says so! You got to be twenty-two inside, too. Anyway, why fuss? You don't love him.' She flickered a sly glance at her daughter.

Corey thought of Jude and wondered how anyone could tell what love was. 'How do you know I don't?'

'You're here, aren't you, not with him.'

'It's not that simple, Ma. He's wealthy. He wants to marry me and for us to live in a massive great mansion. I can't do that.'

'Why.' It was a statement rather than a question.

'How can you ask that! You of all people! Surely you understand what that would mean? I'd have to give up so much of my own life, entertain his friends, maybe travel the world, lose all my freedom.'

'Yes.'

'*Ma!*' Corey jumped up from the folding chair and strode angrily up and down the lay-by. 'Don't you care about me? I have a kind of love for him—I think—but I've got gipsy blood in my body and I can't give up my independence! I won't be shackled by a man—I won't have him organising my life!'

'Shh, my daughter, you'll wake Persalf.'

'Oh, damn Persalf!' shouted Corey in despair.

The caravan door banged open.

'Del! You woke me!' Persalf's eyes focused on Corey in surprise. 'What you doing here? I thought . . .'

'Run away from the man,' observed Rupa calmly. 'That angry man—Wallace's kin. Corey won't marry him. Says she'll be caged.'

Corey turned to Persalf. 'You know what it would be like. You're free to come and go as you choose, you know how marvellous it is. Don't you see my problem?'

Persalf grunted derisively. 'Nobody's free. You live a fancy tale.'

'All gipsies are free,' began Corey.

Rupa took her daughter's hands between her own. 'Listen, my baby, listen good. You know nothing. If we'd been with the tribe, you'd have been married at fifteen, living with your husband's family till you had a child. You'd obey your husband in everything and follow him—maybe round the world. Just like you say you'd have to with this man of yours. No Rom is free like you reckons. For your kind of freedom you must live alone, go without love, be on your own when you're old. You want that?'

'I don't like being told what to do,' sulked Corey.

'No. You never did. Daughter, what are you afraid of? Love? Choose that any time. Not many folk find it.'

'Who says I've got it?'

'I says.' She sighed. 'You be just like me when love came. Like a frightened rabbit, running all ways. I said no to your pa.'

'But that was different. You were both promised to someone else. You couldn't marry.'

'We could. We did.'

'After you got pregnant—after you'd both been beaten,' retorted Corey. 'And you were banished from the whole community for ever. That's the worst punishment that can be inflicted, worse than death. Was it really worth it?' she asked.

Rupa twisted the wire stems into the poppy petals which lay in a brilliant slash of colour on her lap.

'Without the group, a Rom is only half-alive,' she said softly. 'We missed the company something bad.

But I had love every day, every hour that he lived.' The taut lines of her face gentled.

'You never spoke of him,' said Corey.

'Don't call the dead back.'

Corey couldn't let this rare expansive mood go without knowing more about her father. Speaking about him had been taboo. All she knew was that he had died 'from his chest'.

'He was a good man?' she asked.

'Some. Like you, he was. Could be happy and angry and loving all in one breath. Difficult to live with, impossible to live without.' Rupa stretched out her hand. 'Choose love, my baby. Don't let it go.'

'I wish I'd known Pa.'

'He seed you born.'

Persalf watched the range of emotions flitting over her face. 'We all needs someone to love,' he said quietly.

'I've got you,' Corey protested. 'That's enough for me.'

'We travel. We sees you too little,' said her mother.

'I could live with you—I could come with you. My job can be done anywhere. I'd bring in money for us all,' she said excitedly, warming to the idea.

'No. Tell her,' Rupa said to Persalf.

He settled more firmly on his haunches. 'The Kris Romani is meeting about us. You knows what that means?'

Corey did. The tribunal of gipsy elders were going to discuss the Lees' banishment.

'I reckons they let us go back,' he continued.

'There's no reason why I can't come too,' said Corey.

'Huh!!' Rupa and Persalf both gave the same involuntary snort of laughter.

'What's so funny?' she asked, offended.

'You hated the rules before,' observed Persalf.

Corey flushed. She'd forgotten what a restrictive life it was, how many hygiene laws there were and how often she broke them thoughtlessly.

'He's right, you're too flipperty to settle,' said her mother. 'Travelling is hard. I know you work hard, but we has to do things we don't want to. Someone has to do the bad jobs. There's a spoken law for everything we do and no one breaks that law. You'd be trouble. You don't do as you're told.'

'So much for the illusion of gipsy freedom,' remarked Corey bitterly.

'You have more freedom now. Anyway, freedom's inside your head. No one owns your mind. And remember it's only in the water that you learn to swim.'

But could she dare to take the plunge? Wasn't it safer on the sidelines? Corey's frustration rose. She'd come for help, for an answer, and they were abandoning her again, intent only on their own lives.

'He loves you. He'll help,' comforted Rupa.

'She don't know if she loves him, *na*,' said Persalf.

'She's just a child,' explained Rupa. 'You told him about us?' The black sparkling eyes turned full on Corey.

She lowered her lashes. 'Not yet. I've had enough people recoiling from me in the past.'

'You tell him. If he accepts it, he loves you real strong,' said Rupa.

'And if not?'

'Then he's not good enough for my Corey. You need a big man to understand you, my daughter. Maybe another man will come along. Don't be so impatient. Love is worth waiting for. Go and find out, Corey'

'You'll be here, if he rejects me?'

'They be moving us on,' reminded Persalf. 'We go to the Kris Romani.'

'Then I'd be all alone in the world!'

'You wanted freedom,' said her mother, then, relenting, she offered, 'stay till they comes for us. Then go.'

'You never wanted me around you,' accused Corey.

'You think that? I let you go to give you a chance in life. Salf was too much a Rom to change. You *had* to have more than a lonely wandering life.'

'I thought you didn't love me.'

Rupa smiled sadly. 'I loved you too much.'

That was what Newton had told her, one day during the Christmas vacation. She'd curled up in front of the library fire, he was lazing in the huge leather armchair.

'Your mother had to cut off her emotional responses to you, Corey, otherwise she could never have let you leave. You must understand that,' he said.

'If that was true, why didn't she *say* that?' she complained.

Newton re-filled his pipe. 'Wouldn't you have pestered her to let you run wild instead of going to school?' he asked shrewdly.

She smiled. 'I'll say! But it would have been easier if I hadn't been trying to remember the rules of two cultures. I never seemed to get either one right. I was a failure in both.'

'You call it a failure to be studying at one of the best art schools in the country?' he enquired mildly.

'Everyone looks down on the pre-apprentices,' she retorted. 'When will I ever be accepted, Mr Wallace? I was isolated at school, I'm tolerated at college, gossiped about in the village . . .'

'I accept you. Now what we must do is to make sure that *you* accept you and to hell with everyone else.'

'Is that how you see life? I wish I had your strength of mind. You don't seem to care what anyone thinks.'

'I care that my brother-in-law thinks badly of me,' he sighed.

Corey turned in the narrow bunk in the wagon as she remembered the conversation. If only she could face the world with his confidence, then it wouldn't matter who she was, or that there was an insurmountable barrier between herself and Jude.

He had been an insider all his life. Born to money, educated with the élite, he hadn't suffered a continual denial of his rights as a person. Yet ... he *was* unconventional. He had carved his own path. The gap between them was less than it ought to be, given his upper-class background.

Newton had been like him, now she looked back.

He had inched into her confidence with a fine delicacy and taken away the hollow rootless feeling. She belonged to Sedgewood—Newton's Sedgewood. Not Jude's elegant house.

It would be arrogant of her to imagine that Jude saw her as an equal. He had a fortune and could pick any girl he wanted for a wife.

If only she didn't love him! After a day of backbreaking work for her mother, she lay exhausted in the narrow bed, listening to her mother's steady breathing, knowing she must—for once—think things through.

'Tell me about him,' came Rupa's voice.

'You're awake!'

'I can hardly sleep while you toss and turn and sigh.'

'I'm sorry.'

'So. What's bad about him?'

'Lots. Everything. He lives in a different world. He's rich. He's sophisticated, a very clever business man. He's jealous and explosively passionate.'

'That all?'

'It's masses!'

'Huh! Now let's hear the good.'

'He's different; unpredictable, unconventional. His mind is very quick. He's very creative—oh, Ma, you should see his work, you'd love it! He's so sensitive, he sees right into people and captures the essence of them. Even his plans for houses are just right for his clients. And he likes wild gardens, and he loves horses, and he doesn't think wishing is silly, and—oh, I must tell you, there's this amazing picture of me, that ... Ma! You're laughing!'

The bunks were shaking slightly. 'Don't mind me, go on, let me get a picture of this man,' said Rupa, trying to control her mirth. It wouldn't be long before this Jude gentled Corey.

'He makes me laugh,' said Corey quietly, remembering the fun of their conversations. 'He brings me to life, as if he was switching me on. There's something else: I know him. He's as familiar to me as if I'd been with him all my life.'

'That's love,' said Rupa complacently. 'Stop thinking you're fitted to be a Rom, you're not. I was right in what I did, letting you go. You've grown into a grand girl and fallen for a grand man.'

'I've never belonged before. I'm afraid of it. I don't think I know how to adapt.'

'But you have to try, child. You'll find life with this man grows on you, as it did with Mr Wallace. When you dines off silver every day it soon becomes ordinary!'

'I'm going back in the morning.'

'Yes,' said her mother, unmoved.

'I'll leave after breakfast.'

'You'll be back home early, then.'

Corey could never get used to the calm acceptance of anything that happened. Yet their leave-taking, as always, was emotional, for they knew it would be a long time before they saw each other again. The camp would travel all over the country; Salf would marry and she . . . heaven knew what would happen to her.

Two weeks later, she was no nearer solving her relationship with Jude. He had obviously called while she was away, since there was a note from him on her doormat, but his interest had apparently waned quickly because he did not call while she was there, even though she hung around waiting. She did not have the courage to march up to the manor and accept his proposal—it seemed so cold-blooded.

When she had broken off her engagement with Tom, she had enjoyed her independence. Time lay heavily now. Even working flat-out did little to alleviate the loneliness and emptiness that surrounded her. Cat strolled in and out of her life as usual, the hens scratched around contentedly and the bees continued to pollinate the neighbourhood. She caught herself staring emptily into space, or looking yearningly at the Manor, hoping at any moment to see Jude's tall figure striding over the field to claim her.

Restless and unhappy, she took to wandering through the woods, soothed a little by the life around her, sometimes a painful stab catching in her chest when she realised that the world was rolling on quite easily without her. She wasn't needed; it didn't make much difference whether she was around or not.

But she couldn't drift for ever. Reluctantly Corey

settled down to work again, stung by the fact that the shop in Hatton Garden was re-considering her contract. There were many unfulfilled commissions and she would have to work hard to complete them before the promised delivery dates.

On this occasion she was working indoors. It was dull and chilly outside and she had put on a long red cotton skirt and a white full-sleeved blouse with a black waistcoat which hugged her slender waist. Grimly she shaped the silver. This was one design she could have done without! It was to be in the shape of a heart with an arrow through it, the delicate flights and arrow head carrying the initials of a young man and his bride of a year. For some reason, the design was proving extremely difficult.

Tired and hungry, but determined to finish it before the light faded that night, she lit the gas jet and gently heated the metal for the final soldering of the arrow.

Already she had made one mistake on the piece. Dreaming, she had overheated the heart, creating a fire-stain that had taken an hour to file down and re-polish to the original silken finish. She was tired of working on it, but stupidly adamant that it would not beat her; she would finish it. The arrow was put into place.

Just how her heart felt. Pierced. But it wasn't only love that stabbed so painfully, it was the myriad other complications that seemed to arise when two people contemplated getting together permanently. It seemed a miracle that anyone ever married; there were so many factors to be solved. Was it difficult, living with someone else, or was she particularly insular and single-minded?

No longer confident, the doubts crept into her mind. She was inadequate. How could such a wilful, selfish child make a decent wife for any man?

Large tears welled up in Corey's dark eyes, blurring her vision. She directed the blow-torch into the air and rubbed furiously at her eyes till she could see clearly again.

'Oh *no*!' she moaned.

In her reverie, she had forgotten what she was doing and the flame had irretrievably melted the slender arrow. The fine work had taken her most of the afternoon and that evening. She couldn't begin again—she never wanted to see the wretched piece again!

She flung the heart across the room.

'Just look what you've done, Jude Radcliffe!' she cried, dropping the blazing torch in her frustration. Almost instantly, the chintz armchair caught alight. With a cushion, Corey hysterically smothered the flames and turned off the gas jet with shaking fingers.

'Ruined! I can't start all over again, I can't!'

At the end of her tether, unaware that the fire still smouldered on within the chair, she ran out headlong into the twilight, furious that nothing in her life seemed to be going right. She raged along the badger path, teeth gritted and eyes flaming, till she broke out of the wood and began to climb the hill beyond.

A steady stream of cloud hung low on the horizon. Bad weather. Already a strong wind was blowing, suddenly chilling her body which was warm from running. As she slowed with the steepness of the incline, she shivered and lowered her head against the wind. For some reason, she was determined to reach the top of the hill, but it was proving quite a battle. When she crested the summit, the full blast of the wind caught her head on, blowing her backwards and she slipped, grabbing awkwardly at the grass and struggling to her knees.

Corey felt a distinct foreboding as she battled upright and looked down on the other valley. It was virtually dark now, just a few lighter clouds merging with the banks of heaving, rolling blue-black clouds in the sky above.

Far below stretched Sedge Wood, the Manor lands, the village and her cottage. The scene calmed her. Whatever she had thought of herself, she *did* want to settle, in fact she would be reluctant to move from the area. She wanted to get back to the comforts of her cottage and away from this evil wind, even if it meant picking up that damn heart and starting again on the delicate arrow.

Sliding a little, she began the descent, only to stop, sitting down on the slope in her horror.

A black spiral of smoke was rising from her cottage, only just showing against the sky, but visible to Corey's keen eyes.

There was no reason for that, unless . . .

A glow shone in one of the lower windows, where a few moments earlier there had been darkness. Perhaps Jude had wandered in and lit the candles. Perhaps he had made a fire for them. Her heart leapt in hope but still she did not move, sensing instead some disaster and finally seeing to her dismay that the smoke was not coming from the chimney at all, but lower down, as if her sitting room was filled with smoke.

The sight galvanised her into action. It can't be on fire, it can't! I won't let it! muttered Corey to herself, sliding down the hill rapidly, hampered by her long skirt and hitching it up to her waist. Then she stood, and despite the steep slope, ran downwards blindly, falling over and over again, rolling, cursing and

moaning in her mindless need to reach her home and
the loved possessions. The pain of her body was
nothing. She knew it was her fault: obviously she
hadn't put out the flames thoroughly enough. Once
again, her temper and impetuous behaviour had
caused trouble.

She groaned, her mind running through the likely
results of her foolish behaviour. Had she shut Cat
inside? No, the door had been open when she left—
and the window. He'd escape, wouldn't he?

Although she couldn't smell the smoke, as she was
far upwind, there was the awful sight of yellow licking
flames, just beginning to catch the thatch roof. She
clenched her fists, helpless to stop the fire's progress at
such a distance. The fire crawled along the base of the
roof, then, like a rising wave, swept upwards.

The wood had never seemed so large and its
darkness was made worse by the fact that she could no
longer see the cottage. Weakened by her frenzied
climb of the hill and her equally frenzied descent, she
slowed, furious that her legs were so feeble, willing
them to carry her faster. At one stage she almost gave
up hope of ever arriving in time, but at last she only
had the orchard gate to surmount.

Hens were flapping everywhere; she could now
smell the acrid smoke. Gusts of capricious wind
eddied, sending the smoke in her direction, with the
unwelcome heat of the flames. There was a terrible
cracking sound and a popping as if huge blisters were
bursting. She gathered up her skirts again and ran.

For a moment she thought she saw a dark figure,
strangely shaped, like a hunchback. It paused by the
open front door, then it vanished inside and she was
not sure whether she had imagined it or not. Other,
more substantial figures came running, reaching the

garden just before she did. They turned at her wheezing arrival and she gave a little moan of irritation as one of them caught her shoulders, stopping her headlong rush.

'You're here!' he said inconsequentially.

'I'm here!' Corey began to laugh hysterically till the man slapped her face.

'Now, miss,' he said, 'sit down. You look all in.'

It was Jude's gardener, standing anxiously with Silas the groom, their eyes flicking from her to the cottage.

Just then, the wind fanned the flames and in a blistering flare, the front wall of the cottage caught alight, the old horsehair and lime plaster dried by the centuries into a highly combustible material. It crackled like kindling, silhouetting starkly the oak beams and posts which formed the frame of the lodge.

'My things! My workbench—the silver!' moaned Corey.

'To hell with your things,' said the man grimly. He went as close to the burning building as he could. 'Mr Radcliffe! Mr Radcliffe! She's here!'

Corey sat up in shock. Without waiting to hear any more, she dashed for the door, totally distraught. Jude was in there! It was like Dante's Inferno—he'd be cremated!

Before she could run inside, a swift arm snaked out and held on firmly to her wrist.

'No, miss. You can't do anything.'

'Let me go! I must go! He's in there!'

They both leapt back as supporting beams began to crash inside, the flames flaring brilliant yellow-white in response, incinerating everything in their path.

Sparks shot into the air like fireworks, showering over the onlookers.

'You wouldn't survive in there.' Strong arms gripped her securely.

'I don't care! What about him—he'll be burnt alive! Jude!'

Somewhere inside, she could hear his voice. Faintly, it came to her.

'Corey! For God's sake, where are you? Corey!'

'I'm here, Jude, I'm here! Oh!' At the edge of breaking down, she fought the rising panic, crushing the vision of his scorched body trapped under a beam in a futile attempt to find her.

'Corey! Can you hear me!'

'*Jude!* Get out of there!'

'We'll shout together,' said Silas. 'One, two three . . .'

Their shouts must have reached him, for a wild blackened face appeared at the bedroom window, seemingly surrounded by flame. He saw Corey and slumped for a moment against the side of the window in relief, then clambered on to the sill.

Corey ran closer, throwing an arm up to shield her eyes from the furnace blast. Sparks and burning straw filled the air, raining down on her in a hellish tempest.

'Jump, break a leg, it doesn't matter!' she yelled. 'Jump on to me—I'll break your fall! Please, please,' she begged brokenly.

'Here, sir, to the right,' shouted Silas. 'Come back, miss—you'll get burnt!'

He tugged at her and she resisted him, raking her hands at his face. 'Leave me alone! I did it! I should be in there! Jude!'

Her tormented face tore at the two men's hearts as

they fought to contain her and save her from acting foolishly.

It must have taken seconds, but to Corey time stood still. Jude edged along, searching for a soft landing place. But he was taking too long; flames roared around the window, catching his clothes. Before Corey's terrified eyes, he leaped down, framed in flickering fire.

He fell with a solid thud and Corey felt the jarring of his body within herself; she felt his pain. Yet he'd landed on a bed of rhododendron bushes which had broken his fall. Winded, he half-raised himself in a reflex action, then dropped back to the ground again.

Corey knelt by his side, beating out the small licking flames, her body cold with fear despite the scorching heat reddening her face. Behind her, reinforcements from the village arrived, helpless to do anything but haul buckets from her well and fruitlessly hurl them on to the base of the fire. At least they felt they were doing something. With no telephone and no water main nearby, there was nothing anyone could productively do, although the fire engine had been sent for.

'Say something, Jude, anything,' she whispered, her face close to his.

He opened his eyes weakly. 'Ouch,' he said obligingly.

Corey could have beaten her fists against her chest in sheer hysteria.

'You fool!' she cried, burying her head in his shoulder and bursting into tears.

She was pulled roughly away and dragged along the ground, bewilderingly aware that Jude was also being dragged down the garden. In the next few seconds, she heard a dull crash and showers of sparks, flames, dust and smoke covered them all. When the debris settled,

she saw that the whole front wall of the cottage had
blown out.

Jude reached for her and they clung together.

'You all right, sir?' asked Silas anxiously.

'A bit winded.' His voice was hoarse from the
smoke. 'A bit singed here and there. But I'm alive.
And so is she—that's all that matters.' Jude smiled
gently at Corey, her face blackened with soot and
comical with the rivulets made by her tears.

'You ruined my rhododendrons,' she complained,
exhausted.

He grinned, feeling his body cautiously.

'Let's hope that's all I ruined. Are you crying for
your home or for me?'

'You,' she said huskily.

'Ambulance is here, sir,' said the gardener.

'Don't need one,' said Jude, unable to take his
smoke-reddened eyes from Corey.

'No, sir, course not. But shouldn't we see if the
young lady is in shock? You could go with her, as
company.'

The gardener knew his boss well, knew how
stubborn he was, and had recognised the taut line of
chemistry between him and young Miss Lee that day
they had discussed the gardens. Their anguish over
each other in this fire only served to confirm his
suspicions about them both.

Jude helped to usher Corey into the ambulance. She
was past caring what anyone did with her. All she
knew was that Jude was alive and generally
unharmed.

They both refused to lie down, despite the advice of
the ambulanceman who travelled with them, but
during the journey, Jude began to cough violently
from the smoke in his lungs and he was too weak then

to protest when he was tucked up in a blanket and given oxygen. Corey hovered nervously, getting in the way, stroking his filthy sleeves and trembling so much that Jude longed to hold her in his arms again.

'You ought to be lying down too, miss,' said the ambulance man.

'I'm not leaving him,' she defied.

'The stretcher is only two feet away,' grinned the man.

'Please!'

Jude pushed away the oxygen mask and sat up groggily.

'She's stubborn and wilful and I love her,' he said hoarsely.

'Sounds a bit like my wife,' said the man.

'She'll be my wife soon,' promised Jude, his eyes on Corey.

CHAPTER SIX

WHEN they reached the hospital, Corey was trembling uncontrollably. It could have been from shock, or relief, or possibly from Jude's decisive words. Her tired mind whirled with emotions. Jude lay prone, reluctant to speak because of the pain in his throat and lungs.

They were transferred to trolley beds and left in the corridor. Casualty was busy that night. Corey's hand reached out for Jude's. The noises and bustle of the hospital drifted around them as they concentrated on the pressure of each other's fingers. They were both alive. That, for the moment, was sufficient.

When they were wheeled into adjoining cubicles, Corey waited tensely to discover Jude's condition and flew at the doctor with questions immediately he appeared.

'Jude—him next to me—is he all right? Not badly hurt? Tell me what's wrong!'

'Just relax for a moment, Miss . . . er . . . Lee.' He checked her pulse.

'Tell me now.'

'All in good time. So——'

'But I love him—well, not at first, then I—when I found he was in there—I did—well, I nearly killed him, it was the heart, the silver one . . .'

The words were almost incoherent, and the doctor eyed her critically. Corey fought down panic, knowing she must be rational or she'd not be allowed to see Jude. They wouldn't want a demented woman pestering him in his condition. His condition? What the hell was his condition!

Her huge dilated eyes concerned the doctor. 'Gently, gently. Relax. I must examine you.'

'I'm not ill. I ran.' He was directing the nurse to clean up the grazes on her arms and legs and to attend to the bruises. 'Down the hill. I fell a lot.'

'You ran down a hill and fell a lot,' repeated the doctor, shining a torch in her eyes.

'Yes. Oh, it sounds odd, but I'm not drugged or drunk. I saw my cottage was on fire and ran. So would *you*!'

'You fell over?'

'It was dark, damn you!' she raged.

'Leave her alone!' rasped a cracked voice from behind the curtain.

With a muttered exclamation, the doctor disappeared into the next cubicle and spent a little while arguing with Jude and laying down the medical law.

At last Corey was allowed to see him and was horrified at the redness of his face.

'Is your skin burnt?' she asked, wide-eyed.

'No. Heat glare—temporary.'

'I saw flames . . .'

'Overcoat protect. Bad chest—smoke.'

'Overcoat? It's the middle of summer!'

'Been in Rome.' Corey had to strain to catch his words. 'Cold wind after Rome. Put on overcoat, visit you. Saw smoke. Thought—God!' His hands reached for hers. 'You inside.'

'You do love me, then,' she whispered.

'Keep telling you.'

And that was where the porters separated them till the next night. Corey slept all day from the effects of tranquillisers till she was told by the nurses to dress.

When she pulled back the bed-curtains, Jude was there.

'Hello, nightingale.'

She smiled.

'Ready to go home?'

'What home? I haven't got one.'

'Mine. Where else?'

'I couldn't . . .'

'All right,' he said in a matter-of-fact tone.

In helpless bewilderment, she stared. He didn't have to agree that quickly! 'I could find somewhere at the village.'

'You could.'

'Or find a hotel.'

'With a charred cheque book and credit cards?'

'Oh, Lord, I've got nothing! Only—only what I'm wearing! Could you lend me some money?'

He sighed. 'Corey, think straight. Your cottage is burnt down—gutted. It'll take a while to rebuild. You can't afford to stay in hotels. You were insured, I suppose?'

At her anguished look, he gave a deeper sigh. 'Good God, Newton was right. You *do* need looking after. You're like a bloody child!'

'Then I can stay safely with you, can't I—unless you like seducing children!'

Amused sniggers ran around the ward. Corey raised her chin and glared at Jude, totally unconcerned by the disturbance she had caused.

Jude grinned. 'Stay for tonight and we'll sort out your finances. But I warn you, if you show any signs of being a woman, I'll treat you like one. Come on.'

They walked through the ward, not touching, the eyes of everyone on the whip-hard, determined man and the simmering, shapely woman beside him.

Child? they thought. He must be mad. It was obvious what the outcome of their evening would be.

Jude paid off the taxi and was welcomed by Mrs Morris, his housekeeper, who fussed excessively over both of them. The house seemed less intimidating after the bleak, impersonal hospital and Corey was delighted with her room, which overlooked the gardens at the rear. There was a small balcony too, edged by a fat-bellied stone balustrade.

Mrs Morris had left to check on Jude, leaving behind a nightdress and housecoat. Corey didn't have the heart to tell her that she never wore anything in bed, but laid the nightdress carefully on the large easy chair. Most of the furniture was Georgian, in keeping with the house, but it had obviously been lovingly used. Only the bed was modern, though the counterpane was old, a delicately sewn patchwork in pale greens and blues.

Her depression lifted slightly in the pleasant surroundings, though she was too numbed to consider her problems properly. At some stage she would have to visit the cottage and see what could be salvaged, but her physical and mental resources were low right now. For the time being, she would be wise to live from moment to moment.

'If all the house was like this, I could get to like it,' she murmured, idly tracing the stitching on the counterpane.

A knock at the door announced Mrs Morris. 'Excuse me, miss. Mr Radcliffe says . . .' she paused, her eyes raised upwards, trying to remember his exact words, '. . . he wasn't struck on the hospital's idea of macaroni cheese at five o'clock and will you join him for a light supper in the library?' She smiled, apparently used to Jude's eccentric messages.

'Lovely. I *am* hungry,' replied Corey. 'Is it possible—do you think I could have a bath?'

'Yes, miss, course you can, then I'll get together some clothes for the morning. You can't wear those.'

They both looked at the bedraggled, stained garments that Corey had hastily dragged on at the hospital.

'I don't want to be a bother.'

Mrs Morris beamed. 'No bother. Have a nice bath and come downstairs. Mr Radcliffe said supper in the library, so I'll show you where that is.'

The *en suite* bathroom had been totally modernised. Corey's bare feet sank into the thick, comforting, shaggy-pile carpet and she reached for a box of bath oils. Inside were four small brown phials of ginger, peppermint, lemon and geranium. The drops wafted delightfully up with the steam, scenting the air. It was such a luxury to turn on a tap and discover hot water! And an even greater pleasure to lie full length, the silky water lapping gently over her breasts.

The bathroom seemed to contain everything she might want. A frown creased her forehead. Of course, no one knew she was coming until the last minute! All this must be at the ready for any female visitor who happened to take Jude's fancy. Her spirits sank. Could she trust him to be true to her, after a life of gallivanting about?

Wishing she could stay soaking longer, but quite ravenous now, Corey towelled herself dry with the huge, soft green towels, wincing a little when she forgot the bruises on her body and touched a tender spot by accident.

Then she remembered Lydia. The woman would be having dinner with them too. She examined herself critically in the mirror, her face devoid of make-up, an unusual pallor under her dark skin. Well, she'd get dressed and sweep in ... hell! Not even the most beautiful woman in the world could sweep in successfully while wearing Mrs Morris's housecoat!

Corey ran to try it on, experimenting with the neckline, then the sleeves. Faced with the prospect of Lydia staring at her, she decided that this time she would wear the nightie underneath the housecoat as a kind of protection; she quickly pulled on the pink brushed nylon with a wrinkle of her nose in distaste.

The sight made her laugh. If Jude was expecting a bit of rivalry between the two women in his life, he was in for a shock! In this nightie she wouldn't be a contender. It would make things easy for him; he'd choose Lydia to grace his bed without a second thought. Damn her! Dolefully, but half-laughing at her own frumpiness, Corey buttoned up the high neckline and slipped her arms into the housecoat, fastening the zip right to her chin.

'There!' she said, giggling. 'You look like an ad for contraception. 'Ladies, does your husband bother you? Solve all your problems by wearing our anti-sex nightwear.'" Her peal of laughter rang around the room and she hastily shut her mouth, looking around apologetically. It seemed indecent to laugh. Really, she should feel tragic.

Mrs Morris was waiting for her at the bottom of the stairs and showed her into the library, though Corey already knew it well. It was Newton Wallace's favourite room. Jude had put in a few new furnishings, but otherwise had hardly changed it. The walls were completely lined with books, a pale beige carpet covered the floor and a cheerful log fire burnt in the grate. Jude was sitting in a casual open-necked shirt and silver-grey slacks, facing the fire. He indicated for her to sit in the easy chair opposite his.

'My God!' he exclaimed as she slunk into the chair.

'Where's Lydia?' she asked, ignoring his comment.

'Lydia?'

'Oh, come on, Jude, she lives here, doesn't she?'

'Not at the moment. She's in Rome. We went together, and she stayed to do some shopping.'

'How nice,' said Corey, fumingly jealous.

'It was. What in the world are you wearing?'

The corners of Corey's mouth quirked. 'Awful, isn't it? Mrs Morris's night attire. Tell me, is her husband still around?'

'He's the gardener.' Jude couldn't tear his eyes from the outfit.

'That's good. At least he has a choice of beds,' observed Corey.

Jude roared. 'I see what you mean. Was that you laughing when you put this—er—night attire on? I wondered if you'd gone mad, for a moment.'

'It was me laughing.' Corey was disappointed. Wasn't he supposed to think she looked adorable in anything?

'Hmmm. You look very prim. I hardly recognise you.'

'It's still me underneath. Look,' Corey started to raise the trailing hem of the housecoat, to show him her legs, only to stop as Mrs Morris entered with a tray.

'Here we are, Mr Radcliffe. Oh, miss, you do look nice. Now, you both eat up this soup while it's hot, then there's cold chicken and salad and some banana pudding left over from my lunch. And I took the liberty of bringing up a bottle of red wine. Very good in cases like these.'

'Mrs Morris, you've rustled up a feast. You're very

kind. We've kept you up late enough, though. Would you mind locking up for me tonight? Leave the hall lights on and I'll make sure everything is shut up in here. You go to bed now.'

'Right you are, Mr Radcliffe. If you ring down in the morning, I'll bring up breakfasts. What shall I do about the cat? He's fidgeting about outside.'

'Bring him in,' said Jude, smiling.

'What cat? What cat?' asked Corey excitedly. 'Oh!'

In Mrs Morris's arms was a wriggling, protesting Cat. She let him jump down and he suffered Corey's embrace, then shook off her hands and prowled around, investigating thoroughly, before settling down in front of the blazing fire as if he had been there before.

'How did anyone ever catch him?' she asked.

'He was skulking about in the orchard. He gave up his freedom for a tin of salmon,' grinned Jude. 'I got Mr Morris to check on your livestock. The hens were all hysterical, but he shut them up in our coop and they calmed down. The bees, I'm afraid, have all evacuated your orchard and are at present hanging in a pendulous swarm on one of my oak trees in the garden. It seems all the wild creatures from the lodge are here.'

She bared her teeth at him. 'Grrrr! Thanks, that was thoughtful of you.'

'Your room all right?' Jude asked politely.

'Lovely. I enjoyed the new-fangled idea of hot water coming out of taps, too. I get exhausted pumping up enough to fill my bath.'

'I'd have come and pumped water for you any time,' he said. 'And scrubbed your back.'

'Do you always have a room ready with bath oils and tissues and hairbrushes and hairdryers and cotton slippers?' she asked, choosing to ignore his flirting.

'Of course. We have a number of guest bedrooms. Mrs Morris never knows who I'll bring home.'

'I bet she doesn't,' said Corey savagely.

His eyes twinkled as he stacked their soup plates. 'Corey, if I invited back any—er—one-night stands, I can assure you that they wouldn't be in that room, they'd be in my bed.'

'Oh. Yes, of course.' She felt a fool. It was because she had never been in a house where rooms were constantly prepared for visitors. He must think her very gauche. Suddenly she realised that her fork was digging into a piece of chicken. 'Would you like this?' she offered. 'I'm vegetarian.'

'Why?' he asked, spearing the slices on to his plate.

'Moral grounds.'

'Good for you. Myself, on immoral grounds, I could never resist a nice tasty bit of flesh.'

'So I gather,' said Corey drily. 'You've improved this room,' she continued, looking around.

'You're very adept at changing the subject, but thank you. I gather Newton spent a great deal of time here.'

'Yes. And me.' A question was forming on his lips and she forestalled him. 'What other plans do you have for the house? Tell me what you're doing.'

'That would take hours. But basically, I'm repairing, restoring, and trying to decorate tastefully.' He relaxed in the big armchair, crunching on a piece of celery. 'One of my most ambitious schemes is to clear the silted lake. You can see the dip in the ground from your bedroom window—have a look in the morning.'

So he expected her to be still in her bedroom at breakfast time! It would have been flattering if he had tried to seduce her. The housecoat must be more devastating than she thought. It isn't me, only my feathers he likes, she thought miserably.

Jude poured more wine for them both. 'Yes,' he continued, 'I'm rather keen on introducing wildfowl. It would be rather fun to see lots of little chicks or whatever you call them, toddling down the lawn for a swim. What do you think? What brand do I order?'

'It's more a case of them adopting you, once they know you've provided a lake,' said Corey. 'But if you are buying any—well, I suppose mallards—the drakes have green heads and those curly tails—teal, tufted duck—oh, there are loads.'

'I think you'll have to come with me to the bird sanctuary and I'll point at the ones I like. You can tell me their proper names,' he said. 'My dream is to have swans, though. What kind of those do I get? I have a feeling there's more than the white sort in public parks.'

'You'll never introduce the wild ones. They wouldn't stay. Not unless they came of their own accord,' she said slowly, not unaware of the similarity between the swans and herself. 'You'd have the mute swan. It's not wild any longer—more or less domesticated.'

'That sounds all right,' he said softly. 'A wild creature, consenting to live on my lake of its own free will.'

Corey sipped the wine, the glow of the fire and the warmth of the claret inside her brightening her eyes. 'Be wary of them at nesting time. The cob can be violent in defence of his mate and young. He'll attack a man and can break his arm with his wing. You'll love it when the cygnets cadge a ride on the adults' backs.'

They lapsed into silence, their own thoughts flowing fast. The fire crackled and sparked. Why doesn't he make a move? thought Corey. Here I am, available, and he isn't trying. Can he be more hurt than he said? Is he too bruised or burned to contemplate sex? He'd made light of his injuries, but he must be in some pain. Should he have left hospital?

She wasn't sure whether she was glad or not, that he made no attempt to seduce her. Since leaving her mother, she had virtually made up her mind that she would let the relationship develop and decide whether or not to marry him at some later date, *if* they were still together. Now, it seemed, her plans were being thwarted by Jude himself!

Jude, struggling with his conscience, was deliberately crushing the desire he felt for the flushed pink-clad girl sitting so tantalisingly close. He wanted to take her in his arms, ghastly housecoat and all. She looked so defenceless and appealing, curled up in the massive chair, her hair tousled as if she had just woken up beside him in bed. A stab of desire ran through him.

Goddamnit! He must squash his lust. It just wasn't the right time. She must be a mass of emotional distress at the moment. In any case, he couldn't seem to introduce the idea of serious flirtation; he'd tried earlier, but his words had come out too jokingly and she had diverted them carefully.

It seemed she didn't want him. Probably the loss of her house and the vastness of the manor was unnerving her. She was so much a kid really. He looked at her from under his lashes as she stared into the fire with wide eyes.

Except . . . where the hell had she been these last few days? Jude rubbed his top lip hard. She'd disappeared about the same time as that damned gipsy.

He refilled his glass, slopping a little on to the table. No woman could go with an earthy man like that and not end up . . . He pictured them together, naked in a field somewhere. If only she wasn't so untrammelled by normal morals and codes! Most women wouldn't consider the idea of taking off with a gipsy. Corey obviously saw him as a soulmate. And a body-mate, curse her!

With one huge gulp, he finished the claret and stood up shakily.

'I think we should go to bed,' he muttered, his eyes lowered.

Startled brown eyes flickered up to judge his expression and failed.

'I hoped you'd help me decide what to do.'

'What do you mean?' he asked flatly.

'About the cottage. About my bank card and money and silver and tools.' Her voice rose in distress.

'Oh, that. Don't worry, I'll handle all that in the morning. I really think we should go up now.'

'I'll take the tray out,' she offered dully.

'Leave it. I'll just rake the fire. You go on up, I'll turn out the lights. Good night. Sleep well.'

At his dismissive, dull tone, Corey ran her hands through her hair and rose.

'Good night, Jude. I hope you feel better in the morning,' she said quietly.

He turned away, saying nothing in reply, and she quickly hurried out of the room. The wide stairs seemed dauntingly tiring to her exhausted body.

Good thing I'm not trying to make love. I wouldn't have the stamina. I'd be a great disappointment.

Out of sight and hearing, she shut the bedroom door

and leaned against it wearily. It must be the hard work
she'd done for her mother that had taken the stuffing
out of her. Discovering that she was hopeless as a
gipsy had been a hard lesson to learn. She'd always
rather fancied herself as a free spirit, travelling the
countryside. Now she knew that she wasn't skilled
enough to be a Rom. It was quite a shock to her
prestige and romantic nature.

Nor, she sighed, placing the housecoat on a chair
and stripping off the nightdress, nor was she much
good as an ordinary person. Pity. She wasn't going to
be any kind of mistress of this house and she didn't
have any other house to be mistress of. Her future
stretched out blankly.

An hour later, she was still awake; she had gone
past sleep. The wind seemed to have died down and it
was warmer now. Wrapping the quilt around her, she
padded to the balcony and inhaled the rose-scented
air. To her left, against the stone wall, clambered a
yellow tea-rose with purple-tinged foliage, swathing
the wall in blooms. If she leant forwards, she could
just . . .

'Take care,' said Jude's soft voice.

Corey looked around. He had come out on to the
balcony next to her, wearing dark blue silk trouser
bottoms and a blue wrap which hung open, showing
his bare chest. Corey turned away and stretched to
snap the slender stem, straightening up triumphantly.

'Now where are you going to put that?' he asked
wickedly.

When she had reached out, she had allowed the
quilt to gape open. In belated modesty, she clutched it
to her again.

'Where would you suggest?'

She raised one eyebrow at him and he laughed, then

rubbed his lip and went inside. She waited for him to reappear, but he seemed to be ignoring her.

Damn him! She was cold now, too, and wide awake. If his bedroom was the next room along, then maybe it would serve him right if she went in and woke him up to tell him about herself. Then she had nothing to fear from any gipsies who might come to the area; her story would all be out in the open.

That, of course, was the only reason she was making her way to his room.

Not bothering to wait for a reply to her knock, she walked straight in. Jude was not in bed; he was standing in the middle of the room, head bowed in an attitude of dejection. Slowly he raised his eyes and a light dawned in them.

Corey averted her gaze from his tanned chest, forcing herself also to take her mind away from the thought of his strong legs beneath the blue silk.

'I've got something to tell you,' she said huskily.

'About your men?' His eyes raked her face mercilessly. She clutched the quilt more tightly.

'I'm cold,' he said. 'Don't mind if I get into bed, do you?'

Corey shook her head numbly. This was going to be difficult. She sat gingerly on a basket chair near the bed. Jude looked at her expectantly.

'I used to think I was like anyone else,' she began. 'I knew other children had fathers, that mine had died, I knew that other children lived in houses.'

'What do you mean?' he asked, leaning forward in sudden interest.

'It was all so hazy to start with. Gradually I learnt that other children went to school, where they learnt things.'

'You were taught at home, then?'

She continued to evade him, wanting to say it her way. 'When I was eleven, my mother decided I should go to school. It was a shock. Immediately we arrived, they began to make fun of me.'

'Why?'

'I couldn't read or write.'

'Good lord!'

'Ma kept insisting I go and I had to do as she said. She did it for the best. All I could do was draw. They always asked me to draw pictures for their projects, but I wouldn't. So they usually tore up everything I did and I had no work to hand in.'

'Little cows!' said Jude bitterly.

Corey shrugged. 'I know how strange I must have been—half-wild.'

'Wilder than now?' asked Jude in mock amazement.

'Much! The boys were particularly cruel. They discovered that I was terrified they'd touch me and so they persecuted me constantly. I spent most of playtime screaming and fighting. Eventually we were asked to leave. We travelled around a bit, till four years ago, when we were staying a few miles away and I had a silly argument with my mother.'

'That was surely the time you started to work for Newton,' said Jude.

'Yes. He had an unbroken Arab mare and no groom. I came just at a lucky time.'

'You were the reason that Father and I didn't visit Newton,' said Jude wryly. 'When he heard Newton was living with a young girl, they fell out and we were banned from setting foot here—though he still left me Sedgewood.'

'It was all innocent. We became very fond of each other. He got me an apprenticeship with a goldsmith.'

'That's how you learnt your craft,' he remarked.

'Partly. I went on a pre-apprentice course to the Sir John Cass School, where I learnt techniques. Nothing creative, though: we weren't allowed. Apprentices had to stick to trade pieces.'

'Why?'

Corey smiled. 'We were the lower tier of the system and were treated as such. That was our job, to learn a trade, not be creative.'

She thought of her fellow apprentices, many of them Jews, many sporting dreadlocks, and how segregated they all were by virtue of their age, class, education and vocation. The pre-apps. sat at one end of the common room, the more privileged students spread confidently everywhere else.

'Mr Wallace knew I was frustrated so he paid for private lessons in design.' She hung her head. 'It cost him more than I thought, living in London. I had no idea of money; when I needed something, I bought it, and there was always money in my account. He hadn't taught me about finance at all. I realise now how he indulged me. But he seemed to enjoy hearing about my life there.'

'And after your course you returned.'

'Yes. Mr Wallace offered me the cottage free and set me up.' There was a silence. Jude had leaned back against the pillows.

'Just one thing I want to know. This man, the weight-lifter fellow prowling about in the woods . . .'

'Yes?'

'Once you said you'd never let me make love to you—that if you chose a lover it would be someone of your own sort. Is he what you imagine to be your sort? Is that overgrown piece of meat your gipsy lover? Damnation! I'm sorry. I intended to ask you rationally. I can't—I'm only human! Tell me!'

Corey began to smile at the idea, infuriating the already maddened Jude, who swung his legs out of the bed and advanced on her.

'No, Jude, let me . . .'

'Tell me!' His arms caught her and whirled her around, ripping away the quilt. Before she could catch her breath, he had pushed her back on the bed and was pinning her down with his body.

'These aren't the bruises I gave you,' he rasped. 'They're fresh. What a little masochist you are!'

'But I got them when . . .'

'You're not going to tell me the sordid story, surely? I can't give you as much pain and pleasure as he obviously can, but by God I'll try. Did he hold you like this? Did he touch you here? Hell, Corey! How did you enjoy him—in a wood? A forest? By a river?'

Jude's breath was coming hard and fast in her face as she twisted her head from side to side, trying to avoid his mouth and tell him the truth.

'Before I finish with you tonight, I will have enjoyed you in every possible position in every possible place in this house,' he claimed wildly, frantically reaching for her lips. At last he captured them, fiercely working on her mouth, groaning at the pleasure her body was arousing as she writhed ineffectually beneath him.

'And your throat . . .' His kisses fell to her neck and the hollow. 'Your shoulders, your breasts—did he take your breast in his mouth like this? Did it feel as good? Better?'

'Ahhh . . .' Corey shuddered at the sensation. 'Jude, about Per . . .'

'Good, was he? Animal-like? Oh, my God!' he groaned, 'one of these days I'll make love to you the way I want to, not in competition with someone else!'

His mouth swooped down on the rapidly swelling nipple, his hand expertly raising the peak of her other breast till it was as hard and turgid as its twin. 'And his tongue, have ... you like that. How full your breasts are! You are so beautiful, Corey. I can't blame any man for wanting you. You're untamed; passionate. No wonder you respond! But I wish you wouldn't! It tears me inside to think that his hands, his mouth, his tongue, has been here ... and ... here ... and ... aaah!'

'Please, please!' moaned Corey, nearly beside herself with desire.

'You little wanton! It excites you to think of us both. Two grown men, vying for your favours. Remember as I take you, Corey. This is me. Forget your gipsy lover while I'm touching you.'

Corey's head was swirling with delirious sensations as his tongue trailed delicately over her thighs. Jude's hands parted her legs and she gave an involuntary gasp. Then he had moved away from her.

'You're so easily aroused,' he said bitterly. 'I can hardly take credit for it. Maybe I should leave you to your lonely bed. I'm not honestly keen on sharing my women, Corey.'

'I'm not one of your women!' she blazed.

'That's obvious. But I'm one of your men.'

'You really think that?'

'What else can I think? Kissing gipsies in the middle of a wood is hardly the action of an innocent.'

'I'm glad you're jealous,' she purred.

'Jealous! I can hardly contain myself. I want to rape you and hurt you and I want to love you and hold you tenderly. You mix me up. You lie there with your black hair spread all over my pillows and look at me with your seductive eyes and I melt into a helpless mess. I hate being your prisoner. I think you'd better go back to your own bed—I'm in too much of a state.'

She was damned if he was going to arouse her and send her off, frustrated. She leaned over him, the heat of her body making him shiver. The full swell of her breasts, close to his lips, maddened him.

'Tell me about Lydia,' she teased huskily. 'Did she touch you here, and . . . here . . .'

'Corey! You bitch! Don't . . .',

'Did her mouth capture your nipple and . . .'

Her voice was lost as she chewed gently. This time, Jude's shudder was from desire. He spread his fingers in her hair and she nibbled his chest, then ran her tongue around every curving muscle there.

'Come up here,' he commanded.

'Only if you're gentle with me,' she pouted.

He moaned and gritted his teeth. 'I don't know if I can control myself. I've always prided myself on my technique,' he said as she began to slip her tongue over his shoulders and up the whipcords of his neck. 'You just make me go overboard. If I don't hold back, forgive me,' he whispered. 'You're driving me crazy!'

'Good,' she murmured. 'It's lovely to have such power.'

'You're wicked, enjoying your hold over me. Maybe I should show you who's boss around here.'

'Mmmm,' she agreed, 'I'd like that.'

Impatiently, he reached out for her, but she evaded his grasp and slid laughing on to the floor.

'All right, that's as good a place as any,' he growled, as she tried to crawl away.

'Let go my foot!' she cried, trying to wriggle her ankle from his firm grasp.

Jude had hauled himself up to cover her with his body, pressing his weight full upon her. She felt the hardness of his chest and thighs and how highly aroused he was. He began to move against her and she moaned in her throat.

'I want you naked,' she breathed in his ear. 'I want to feel you.'

With an indrawn breath, he slid off his pyjama trousers and forced his body hard down again. But the rest of his movements were slow and languorous, his eyes and mouth, tongue and teeth caressing in infuriatingly slow insistent rhythms, his voice huskily arousing her, his whole body slightly sliding and moving now against her silken skin, outlining each rib with the journey of his mouth.

She had no conscious thoughts; her mind had been submerged by a more primitive part of her subconscious. Her head began to sway from side to side and she moaned gently, demanding that he should stop the gentle seduction and take her.

'Not yet,' he whispered.

'Mmm. Now, *now*!' she groaned.

'A little more here ... and I stroke you ... there. You're not ready.'

'I am, I am!' she protested. She couldn't stand it any more; all her nerve endings had reached explosion point.

'Slowly, slowly,' he urged.

He had left her and slithered downwards, searing a path of fiery open-mouthed kisses, his moist warm mouth so sensitive, finding an immediate response in every part of her body. As his tongue caressed her hips, she opened her thighs invitingly, thrusting her pelvis upwards, demanding his attention.

'Touch me, feel me, cover me, take me,' she whispered huskily.

His mouth moved to the soft inner part of her

thighs, touching so lightly that she strained to feel their touch.

'This is where you are warm, where your pulses beat,' came his muffled voice. He struggled to keep a tight control on his stark hunger.

'Damn you, damn you! I can't take any more!' she moaned, twisting her hands in his hair and yanking hard. Unresisting, Jude slid up her body again, his eyes charcoal black, glazed with passion. He cupped his hands under her buttocks and lifted her pliant body. His mouth descended and she welcomed him as he began, with short arousing thrusts, to fill her need. Then he paused.

'No, no, no,' she moaned.

'Shall I go on?' he asked.

In answer, she raked her nails down his back and he arched in shock, then pinioned her hands above her head while he moved, then stopped, then moved again uttering small grunts of pleasure that came from deep within, until her head was swimming and she could do nothing to prevent the tides of tightly strung nerves from breaking, only to be re-heated by his ardour and skill, again and again and again, washing through her brain and through her body in swathes of passion and pleasure until they were both spent in a mutual exhaustion and lay side by side on the floor.

After a long time, she began to nuzzle his neck, little spent moans escaping from her swollen lips.

'Good?' he murmured.

'Mm.'

There was a long silence. Corey could feel Jude's body tensing beside her.

'Whassmatter?' she said lazily.

In answer, he drove his fist into the floor, again and again.

'It's no good, Corey. I can't cope. I've got to ask you. I feel like a schoolboy, but I've got to know!' His voice sounded desperate.

'Know what?' She raised herself on one elbow. What on earth was the matter?

'Him. The gipsy. Was he . . . was he better than me?'

'Oh! Didn't I tell you?'

'*No!* Of course you didn't!' Jude's face loomed over hers, raging.

'You distracted me,' she said. 'Persalf. He's my brother.'

'Your . . .' In shock, Jude sat bolt upright. 'What did you say?'

'You remember, at Tom's dinner, saying our names were middle European or something.'

'But he kissed you, on the lips. He didn't look at you like a brother.'

'Rom kin—gipsy kin—greet each other like that.'

'Kin? Wait a minute, he's a gipsy.'

'Yes, Jude. If I am, and he's my brother, of course he's a gipsy.'

'You never said you . . .' His voice trailed off and a stunned look froze on his face.

'I did, didn't I?' Corey couldn't remember. Jude's lovemaking had taken over all her thoughts. Maybe she hadn't mentioned the word. She'd meant to.

'A gipsy.' Jude's inscrutable face frightened her. Was he going to recoil from her, after being so close, so mad for her?

'Yes,' she muttered.

'I see.'

There was another long silence. They lay on their

backs, staring at the ceiling till Corey shivered. She felt ice-cold, inside and out.

He knelt beside her and picked her up, carrying her to the bed and tucking her up.

'Sleep, my little one,' said Jude softly.

'But . . .'

'Shh! Sleep.' Corey would never have believed that anyone could put so much tenderness in one word. Happily, she stretched her length along the sheets. The warmth enfolded her and the throbbing of her pulses took over her brain, sending her into a deep sleep. Dimly she was aware, just as she drifted off, of Jude sliding in beside her and she curled up contentedly. In the night she half woke and reached for him, but he seemed to be sleeping too far away. It didn't matter. He was there. She slept.

When the morning sun shone so brightly through the curtains that it woke her, she found that he was not lying next to her, nor was there a dent in the pillow where his head would have lain. But there was a note.

It said that he had gone to Spain. It said that until her cottage was habitable, she could live in the Manor and that he had arranged a loan so she could establish herself again. It advised her to go back to her mother and brother, where she truly belonged, for she'd never find happiness in the restrictions of society.

'Oh God!' thought Corey. 'He couldn't take it, he really couldn't accept my background!' She'd thought their relationship was ready for the revelation, but her intuition had proved to be wrong. He had recoiled from her, like all the others.

'You didn't even have the nerve to tell me to my face,' she whispered, still unable to believe that her tender lover could be so shallow.

Then, staring at the note, she noticed the final, cold

gesture. The note was unsigned.

CHAPTER SEVEN

IT was not until the plane was way over France that Jude allowed himself to examine his actions. Until then, he had been functioning on auto-pilot, afraid he would not have the courage to carry out his intentions if he paused to consider.

With the in-flight routine over and the passengers left to their own devices, Jude was forced into an unwelcome solitude and contemplation. The realisation of what he had done hit him like a brick. He had never acted so irresponsibly in his life. It had been a flight of raw instinct. Corey's habits were catching, he told himself wryly.

That night, as she lay beside him, a flash of blind unreasoning panic had swept through his mind. Panic and love. He was virtually enslaved by this wild creature, who lay sprawled in abandon, her tumbling, blue-black hair feathering out in wild sprays across his pillows, her face soft and vulnerable. He had lifted himself gently to gaze on her thick black lashes, and pouting mouth and longed to cover those soft lips with his and claim her again.

She had kicked away the restricting sheet and the lines of her brown body lay tantalisingly curving, awaiting his touch. It was like a disease with him. He couldn't keep his hands off her. He had bitten on his lower lip, the panic surging up as he saw in his mind another woman, dark, passionate, olive-skinned. He must get out as fast as possible.

It was the first time in his life that he had run away.

Always before he had met problems head on. This one was beyond him. That final revelation had clinched it, of course. Now he could see the resemblance between the painting of Corey and the one of his mother. Corey didn't have the same aquiline nose, nor the calculating, wicked eyes or straight hair. But he must have been blinded by Corey's personality not to have realised she had gipsy blood. Certainly her temperament fitted with that of a gipsy.

He glanced at his watch. She'd be waking up now. God! He leaned back against the head rest and a small groan escaped from his lips as he imagined her reaction. There wouldn't be much of his bedroom left when she finished with it. Small price to pay.

All the time he had dreaded this parting, hoping beyond hope that Corey would settle and that his fears were unfounded. Fool that he was! It had been on the cards of course. She: wayward, feckless, inconsistent, glorious. He: both wanting her and yet aware of the potential disaster in such a relationship. He'd been mad to propose—she might have accepted! Neither of them had conquered the devastation of their childhood sufficiently to consider marriage.

His eyes clouded as he remembered the fabulous, untamed woman who had been his mother. Only once had he seen her. It had been in southern Spain, where he lived with his father. Normally dancing in Paris, Rome and Madrid, she had begun a European tour which had opened in her home city of Granada, where the Gitano gipsies had lived for generations. It had been impossible to avoid the posters advertising her presence.

That Christmas holiday was already proving difficult. His father continually complained about his eccentric behaviour at school. Jude was feeling defiant, rebellious. He had succumbed to intense curiosity. He must see the woman who had dominated his childhood by her very absence and whom he obviously followed in personality.

Without his father's knowledge, he had sneaked out of the house, walking up and down outside the theatre for nearly an hour in a bitter January wind before he dared to enter.

The experience had stunned him. Catalina, dancing under her stage name of La Gitana, projected elemental raw sex so powerfully that the cast and audience were mesmerised by her, following every move, every flick of her skirt and slant of her eyes. While he shrank deeper into his seat, shocked that his mother should be carrying on in such a blatantly abandoned way, he became more and more embarrassed at the staring eyes and knowing smiles of the men all around. He was aware of their tension and miserably aware of their desire. Sickness welled in his stomach and he left abruptly, drawing angry hisses for the interruption. For a long time he roamed the streets, never feeling the icy gale which chilled his bones.

Grudgingly, he could admit that if all those men tonight coveted his mother, it was possible for his father to have been captivated too, rousing bewildering and overpowering emotions in a man unused to direct sensuality. No wonder Uncle Newton had also fallen for her. His aunt—newly pregnant—must have been infuriated, even if Catalina was totally uninterested in Newton.

But why did his father marry her? The mores of the time? And why did she marry him? Jude had thought of his gentle, artistic father as objectively as he could.

He was handsome, yes; gifted, sensitive and courteous. Maybe Catalina had loved him. Nothing that adults did would surprise him at that moment.

It made no difference to the fact that it had been a mistake, though. Catalina's frequent affairs and casual disappearances had virtually numbed his patient, gentlemanly father. It was obvious to Jude that he had loved her too much. Once she knew he was enslaved, she had lost interest.

'Excuse me, sir, would you put your table down?'

Jude opened his eyes to see a stewardess hovering close to him with a plastic tray. He shut his eyes again, blotting out the bright, immaculate woman.

'No lunch, thanks,' he said shortly.

'It's very good, sir, chicken salad . . .'

'*No!*' Damn their chicken salad. He'd had enough chicken salads for a lifetime.

'Are you all right, sir? Can I get you a drink, or something? You have a headache?'

Headache! Why wouldn't she leave him alone? 'I don't need anything,' he snapped. 'Wait a minute. I'll have a whisky—double.'

'Yes, sir. Right away. You're staying in Malaga, sir?'

Jude frowned and met her eyes, seeing in them more than polite solicitude. The stewardess was very pale-skinned, with ash-blonde hair and pale blue-grey eyes. You couldn't get further away from Corey with a woman like that. His eyes travelled down her body and she shifted encouragingly.

'Granada.'

'Oh, shame. I thought we might be in the same hotel.'

Aching for Corey, his nerve endings still singing from the last night, Jude stretched out his body, unconsciously sending signals to the girl. They weren't for her; just a reaction to his thoughts.

Jude shut his eyes grimly. He didn't want her.

Poor Corey. She was as passionate and unreliable as his mother, and as unlikely to settle down. The whole essence of gipsies was their wandering nature. It was surprising that Catalina had stayed two years even. You couldn't keep someone like that in a house with a young baby. His parents had been fools to imagine the marriage would work. He wasn't going to be such a fool.

Running a distracted hand through his hair, he caught the glance of an attractive woman, across the aisle. She smiled invitingly and he dropped his eyes quickly. Rapacious creatures, women. God, how he wanted Corey!

Equally distraught, Corey lay for a long time in the bed she had shared with her lover, totally numbed by his shattering desertion. Love. She thought he loved her. So much for its enduring nature.

Despite all he'd said, all his protestations, Jude had used her, enjoyed her body and finally spurned her in a gesture of devastating contempt. It had been that final revelation, of course. All the time they were making love, she thought he knew about her background. Or did she? What unconscious fear had made her miss out the one word that would make him recoil? How dared he persecute her for her birth! What right had he to consider himself better?

'You hypocrite, Jude Radcliffe! You prim, small-minded upper class bastard!'

A pillow went flying across the room. The 'thunk' of it against the wall was vaguely satisfying.

'You coward!' A second pillow smashed into an

occasional table. 'You yellow-streaked whingeing *poseur*!'

By now all four pillows were distributed around the room, settled in debris. She sat up, grinding her white teeth together in blind fury, her hot blood aroused.

'Nightingale! I'll give him nightingale!'

She reached for the bedside lamp and tore it from its socket.

In savage ferocity, she leapt out of bed and tore off the bedding, rending it apart with her strong fingers.

'And this . . .'

The mattress was upended and there began a scene of unmitigated violence as Corey released the emotions which had built within her since she had met Jude, those emotions which had been unbalanced by rejection and which were erupting into an uncontrollable fury.

'Miss Lee, Miss Lee!' The housekeeper stood at the door aghast at the chaos in the room and the black-haired virago in its midst.

'Oh, Mrs Morris!' Corey sank to her knees, crouching as small as she could, covering her head with her arms and rocking, rocking, in floods of tears.

'You poor little thing,' soothed Mrs Morris. Her warm arms curled around Corey in comfort and she settled beside her, murmuring and patting soothingly until the tears subsided.

'He's gone! He's left me!' moaned Corey.

'I know. He'll be back.'

'He won't! You don't understand!' she cried wildly.

'We'll see. I think you'll find he can't keep away from you. I've looked after him for years, Miss Corey,' the housekeeper raised Corey's chin so that she was forced to look at her, 'and I've never known him so happy. There's been lots of women, that I can't deny. But you're special.'

'I am,' said Corey miserably. 'I must be the first gipsy in his bed.' Deliberately she stated the fact, waiting for the reaction. For evermore, she was going to announce her position, so that she knew where she stood with people.

'Oh, I know that,' said Mrs Morris, surprisingly. 'That's why you're special. Suit him down to the ground, you do.'

'Then why has he gone?' wailed Corey.

'Men get a bit frightened when their feelings get too much for them. I expect that's what it is. You stay here with me like he told me you would and we'll wait for him to come back.'

'You really think so?' She was prepared to believe anything.

'Well, he can't do without *me* for long. He likes my pies too much.'

Corey smiled through her tears.

'And if he comes back to me, then he'll find you. All right?'

She nodded. 'Couldn't I ring him—do you know where he is?'

'I know, but I promised not to ring. I promised faithfully not to tell you where he was. He needs a bit of time, I expect.' Mrs Morris really believed that Jude was going to talk over the situation with his father. She knew nothing of Jude's mother, since he never spoke of her. In her opinion, men always saw the sense in marriage eventually, however nervous they were when the likelihood of settling down first struck them.

'I'm not used to waiting,' muttered Corey.

'Do you good, then. There's lots to do here. You can help if you like.'

And so she did. She and Mrs Morris settled into comfortable companionship, baking, freezing, discussing the décor of the Manor and walking down together to see the progress being made on the lodge cottage. At night, Corey resolutely shut out any thoughts and forced herself to concentrate on sleep. Some nights it was impossible. Her mind whirred with imaginative scenarios, planning for the day when Jude returned, but that day never came and her impatience grew until one shocking day when she discovered for sure that she was pregnant.

How could he have been so careless! she raged. She didn't want a child—she was still living life, she didn't want to be hampered.

Hiding her condition from Mrs Morris, Corey moved back into her house as soon as she could, explaining away her haste by emphasising her independent nature.

'I love it here,' she said, looking around the manor hall as she prepared to leave, 'but I love my home more. I'm not far. I'll pop back to see you. And I have all the planting to supervise, for the lodge gardens.'

So she had left the housekeeper who had acted as a surrogate mother for her over the past two months. It was now the beginning of October. Season of mists and mellow fruitfulness, she thought drily. Trouble is, I'm ripening up a bit too well. Still no Jude. It was obvious he wasn't coming back to her. What contempt he must feel! She had misjudged him, thinking he was an unusual man. He was too aware of his own position as a gentleman to contemplate a life with her. If only she had faced that fact straight away; all this waiting and hoping had only brought about more pain in the end.

Depression set in over the early winter months.

Grey surroundings always made her miserable and her own mourning made the days seem greyer and drearier. Images conjured themselves up in her fertile mind to mock her of Jude's body, hovering above her, love and desire in his eyes. Her grief took the alternate forms of abject misery and anger, the latter resulting in some extraordinarily aggressive designs. And soon, as her pregnancy advanced, she was unable to conceal it any longer.

'They're talking about you in the village,' observed Mrs Morris one day, as Corey worked on the herb garden at the Manor.

'That's nothing unusual,' she said sharply.

'They reckon you're pregnant by one of those gipsies who were here in the summer.'

'Oh, do they?'

'Corey, I tried to ring Mr Radcliffe last night. I thought he ought to know.'

She rounded on Mrs Morris fiercely. 'That's not fair! I asked you not to! I *asked* you!'

'I know. But you're both acting so silly. It wasn't any good, anyway,' she added gloomily. 'Mr Radcliffe senior said he'd gone to America to live and wasn't giving his address to anyone.'

The news came as a terrible blow to Corey. In the back of her mind she had always hoped . . .

'I'm to shut up the Manor and keep the flat in London,' added Mrs Morris.

'Oh no!' Corey caught her hand. 'I don't want you to go. You're my friend.'

'It's my job,' the housekeeper replied gently. 'You must make a life for yourself, Corey. Why don't you move? There must be painful memories here.'

'Yes. But good ones too. I want my child to grow up here.'

'The villagers . . .'

'I don't care about them. They'll soon forget. It's something exciting to gossip about now, that I tumbled in the hay with a gipsy boy. I'm sorry the Manor will be closed. It ought to be lived in. I'll keep the gardens for you; I don't want them to become overgrown again.'

'Shall I come down after your baby's born?' asked Mrs Morris gently.

Corey reached out to the older woman and grasped her hand. 'Yes. I'd like that very much.'

'Maybe I should get in touch with your family.'

'Difficult,' said Corey wistfully. 'They're somewhere in Austria at the moment. Persalf sent me a letter. I'm designing a present for his wedding.'

Designs and hard work featured strongly in her life now. She had the chance of an exhibition in Paris and was determined to succeed, for her unborn child's sake. Tom rang once, but she made it clear that she wanted to be left alone. Any affection or friendship would only open up her emotions again. She mustn't allow herself the luxury of being close to anyone. Lonely, without the warmth of human contact, she withdrew into herself and concentrated on her career and her baby. She wasn't afraid of the birth; no physical pain could be worse than the agony that tore into her heart.

During every step she took, the sights, smells and sounds reminded her of Jude and sliced anew through her body. The chair where he'd lounged, the gate where they'd first kissed, the badger set, the roses, the orchard where she'd wished for his love—all these inflicted instantly powerful images of him. In her isolation she constantly re-ran their conversations and actions, torturing herself with wishing and dreaming.

Yet she refused to leave and lose all those reminders, so bitter-sweet were they. She grew to love passionately the greatest and most constant reminder of him—their child. Daily it grew within her body, making demands which took her in a compensatory direction. Corey gradually slowed in pace, becoming more gentle and tender.

Often, when she had no wish to work, she would curl up and read one of the many baby books she had purchased and which lay scattered around the cottage. There was a growing unity with the child. As it stretched a tiny arm or leg, announcing its presence, she talked to it, promising days of picnics and pleasure, of meetings with Ma and Salf, of a life in close harmony with nature—all the delights she could imagine.

Jude's child. She hugged the thought to herself. But time and time again she agonised that she would never see the man she loved, adoring and wondering at the sight of her newly born baby.

Early in March, Mrs Morris had come to the Manor. She needed to check the state of the linen and furnishings and to air the rooms. Corey had been invited to lunch, but while they relaxed in the library, making plans for her future, she doubled over in pain.

'My dear! Is it the baby?'

She nodded weakly.

'Wait a bit. We'll see if you really are having contractions. It's early, isn't it?'

'Perhaps it's impatient, like me, poor kiddie,' said Corey ruefully.

'False alarm, I'm sure. Not unusual with a first baby,' said Mrs Morris.

However, it was no false alarm. The housekeeper quickly telephoned Corey's doctor, knowing by the decreasing gaps between contractions that there was no time for any ambulance to get her across country to hospital.

'Come on, pet, up we go. Let's slide some sheets on to the bed in the room you used before, shall we? You liked it there.'

Keeping up a chatter, Mrs Morris helped the gasping Corey upstairs and settled her in the bed, tucking her up like a child.

'Don't go,' pleaded Corey.

'Poor little lamb—no one to be with you but me! It's not right.'

'You're my friend.'

'Friend! You should have the baby's father here, doing his duty,' Mrs Morris said sharply.

Corey winced and was immediately distracted by another, stronger pain. She breathed deeply, concentrating, shutting everything from her mind but the safe delivery of her child. She was so engrossed that she didn't hear the bell, or notice Mrs Morris leaving, until she saw the doctor's face hovering above hers.

Within the hour, she held her child in her arms. A son. Corey smiled at his lusty yells and put her lips close to his ear, whispering his secret name so that the devil could never call him.

'Jude,' she breathed. 'Your name is Jude.'

A tiny hand flailed in the air and caught her proffered finger, gripping tightly. An expression of peace fell on the crumpled little face and she had to overcome a passionate urge to squeeze him tightly with joy. In awe, she smoothed back the mass of black curls and lightly touched the long black lashes which had closed in sleep.

'He's perfect,' she said softly.

'Course he is, pet,' said Mrs Morris, sniffing at the scene. 'What will you call him, then?'

'Kal,' answered Corey, looking at her son with such love that the doctor too was affected and cleared his throat loudly, turning to busy himself with his bag. 'It's after my tribe, the Kalderash. They're metalworkers,' she explained.

'Well now,' said the doctor. 'We'll have to get you into hospital, young lady.'

'No! I want to ... I'll go home,' she said. She dreaded the thought of summoning up enough energy to do so, but she couldn't stay at the Manor—Mrs Morris had to leave in two days.

'You know we can't have you all alone in that cottage of yours,' reminded the doctor. 'That's why you were supposed to have your baby in hospital.'

'Then she's staying here with me,' said Mrs Morris firmly.

'I couldn't ...'

To everyone's ears, there was such an element of yearning in Corey's voice that it was plain she badly wanted to be cared for.

Mrs Morris smiled. 'You don't think you're cheating me of a chance to have fun with that little scrap, do you? You wouldn't be so cruel!'

Corey smiled in exhausted relief. 'So long as I'm doing you a favour,' she murmured drowsily.

They stayed together till Corey was strong again and eager to try caring for Kal on her own in the cottage. Mrs Morris called to say goodbye. In half an hour the taxi would call to take her back to London and the Manor would be empty again.

As she walked down Corey's path, the housekeeper

turned frequently, till Corey was hidden from view. For a long time she carried the memory of the gentle young woman, looking so brave and beautiful, clutching that tiny, precious bundle in her arms. Men! she thought crossly.

CHAPTER EIGHT

TOM! How lovely—I haven't seen you for ages. Come in out of the rain.'

Corey hustled in a sun-bronzed Tom, who kissed her cautiously and carefully slipped off his raincoat for her to hang in the small hallway.

Automatically he removed his shoes and Corey watched in patient amusement as he placed them neatly, their heels in perfect alignment.

'Must keep your carpet nice,' he stated.

'Of course,' agreed Corey. 'Come by the fire.'

'Bad manners, not letting you know I was coming,' said Tom awkwardly. 'But I thought you might try to avoid me.'

'Not now. I've got over my recluse period.'

'That's a relief. You look great,' said Tom admiringly.

'A bit fat,' she confided. 'All this contented living. And eating up scraps from plates. I've developed a mad passion for rusks! This is the culprit, this is the chap who has led my stomach astray.'

Tom followed her gaze and saw her son in the corner of the room, contentedly stacking large wooden bricks with his plump little hands. He noticed the darkness of his hair and the healthy tan. A strong, sturdy child.

'He's great, too,' he said uncertainly. He didn't know much about children.

'Help Kal make a tower while I make us some tea— and I've just baked a crusty loaf. Would you like toast

164

and home-made damson jam?'

'Oh, would I! I've been in Turin. Italians *will* always serve Italian food.'

'Idiot! You've missed your boiled beef, dumplings and roly-poly pudding, have you?'

'I have, I have,' he agreed, cautiously bending down and picking up a brick. To his surprise, his interference was instantly accepted. Kal waved another brick at him and they both settled down to the serious business of perfect balancing.

Corey carried over the tray of tea and set it down on the rug in front of the fire, sliding a plate of quickly cut bread on to her lap and spearing a slice with the toasting fork. She watched the two of them, both deeply concentrating, frowning a little with the importance of the job in hand. Her son had never known a father. She gave an inward sigh. She hoped the lack wouldn't retard him emotionally. It was no problem now, but she was concerned for the future.

'Here,' she said, deftly buttering the slice. 'Put your own jam on. Kal! I've got a biscuit for you.'

Kal looked up at his mother's voice and beamed, crawling towards her and reaching up a brown hand for the biscuit, Then returning to his task.

'Serious little chap, isn't he?' said Tom. 'You ought to be thinking about his education.'

Corey hid a smile. 'Did you get that gorgeous tan in Italy?' she asked, diverting him.

'Yes. I've been there these last three months. It was a bit of a surprise. Radcliffe's are expanding in Europe and their overseas department decided they needed someone to make costings. I've been worked off my feet.'

'Me too. I don't notice the passing of time, I'm so busy. J—Kal keeps me active most of the day, and of course I work whenever I can.'

A crash of bricks made them look around and they laughed at Kal's delighted face as he sat surrounded by the remains of his tower.

'Let's put him to bed and we can catch up on news. I must tell you about my Paris exhibition,' said Corey.

'Paris! Sounds splendid. Um . . . is this putting-to-bed business difficult?' Tom asked warily.

'Pick him up while I collect a few things,' she said. 'Take him upstairs and start undressing him.'

'I'm a stranger . . .'

'Oh, he won't mind. He loves everyone. I have to prise him out of the arms of half the villagers when we go shopping.'

'Really? They never used to be so friendly towards you.'

'It's Kal. He's a charmer. In the summer he'd sit in his little pram in his white sunsuit, beaming his beatific smile, opening wide those black eyes and waving his little brown arms about, and everyone fell in love with him. People are suckers for babies,' said Corey happily. Life had been much easier with her son to bridge a few gaps.

Tom bent down, and Kal stretched out his arms. Tom had never been interested in babies before, but the openness of this child enchanted him. He carefully picked up the warm sturdy boy, who wrapped his arms confidingly around his neck and stared at him solemnly from under his long black lashes. A small lump came into Tom's throat and he cleared it loudly, causing Kal to laugh and pat Tom's mouth.

'See what I mean?' smiled Corey, noticing Tom's enslavement. 'Come on, let's sort him out.'

It took a while to bath Kal and put him to bed because Tom insisted on helping. Eventually, they returned and Corey made a fresh pot of tea while Tom toasted more bread.

The rain drummed down outside relentlessly as she related the success of her Paris exhibition. Tom saw in her a new inner confidence and a gentleness that she had not possessed before. Though her eyes! An emptiness had replaced the dancing life he had once seen there.

Just as he was trying to find a way to manoeuvre the conversation into more personal areas, they heard the unusual sound of a car squelching through the puddles in the lane. The engine stopped and they waited expectantly but no one could be heard on the path to Corey's door. Tom rose, puzzled, and peered through the window.

'Someone's parked behind me in the lane. Don't recognise the car. Know anyone with a BMW?'

'No, I don't. Perhaps they're lost, or it's some salesman calling and he's waiting for the rain to stop.'

'He'll have a long wait.'

Tom shrugged and returned to his toast, slumping down comfortably and stretching out his long legs to the fire.

The bell rang and Corey started, then smiled. 'I never can get used to that sound,' she said. 'This new-fangled electricity. Oh!'

'Hello, Corey,' said Jude's voice, husky with emotion.

For a moment, she stood in shocked surprise while the rain poured down on his bared head. All her dreams had been filled with this moment, of Jude returning and opening his arms wide to her, of their ecstatic reunion.

'Oh, Jude!' she breathed.

For long, lengthening, heartstopping seconds, they

stood devouring each other.

'Corey? You're letting in the rain,' called Tom.

In an instant, Jude stiffened and seemed to shrink. His facial muscles sagged and his eyes dropped away from hers. Damn Tom! Jude began to turn away. Desperately, Corey grabbed his arm and pulled his listless body inside.

'Just look at you!' she scolded softly, trying to even up her breathing. 'Whatever made you come without a raincoat?' In attempting to cover up her reaction, her voice had become sharp. 'Your suit is sopping wet. Take off your jacket and let me hang it to dry.'

As he handed it to her, he did so just as he did that day in the forest. Their eyes locked; they were both remembering.

'Here, I'll hang it up,' offered Tom helpfully.

The moment had been broken again. Corey was disturbed at the way Jude looked. Without his jacket, he wasn't the Jude she had known. This was a thin, ill stranger; tanned maybe, but with taut stretched skin over ridged bones and deep-sunk eyes. Her heart ached for him and she drew him to the fire.

Murmuring a wintry greeting to Tom, he stood with his back to the roaring fire, steam rising from his once-immaculate black pinstriped trousers which were now creased and splashed with mud.

His gaze swept around the room, taking in the scene of Tom reclining in his stockinged feet, buttering a piece of burnt toast, Cat curled up on the arm of Tom's chair, the room strewn with evidence of a cosy family life. And baby toys. Nappies. Little woollen jackets.

He gave a sharp intake of breath in pain and Corey looked at him anxiously.

'Jude, are you ill?' she asked.

'No. Sorry,' he said tightly, struggling to keep his

feelings to himself. This was a terrible blow. He had come . . . He clutched at the mantelpiece for support. No one had warned him of this arrangement. It had never crossed his mind that Corey would have married Tom so soon after his departure and had his child. Tom, of all people! She might as well have married him! For a moment, at the door, he thought he had seen hope leap into Corey's eyes. Perhaps it had, but he could hardly encourage it now.

His agonised realisation that he couldn't live without her, the long conversations with his father and the conclusions he had come to, all these had come too late. In halting, pained words, his father had set his own immature romanticism against Jude's emotional maturity and experience, convincing him that Corey was different to Catalina. But the process had been too slow. All or nothing, Corey once said. Tom now had all.

He had to get out. He couldn't stand this happy domestic atmosphere.

'Sorry,' he continued. 'I've intruded.' He turned, suddenly aware that his wet shoes were leaving marks on the carpet. 'Sorry,' he mumbled again. 'I should have checked . . .'

'Don't go,' said Corey huskily. 'We're having some tea. Please stay for a cup.'

'No, I . . .'

'Of course you must,' said Tom heartily. He'd never seen Radcliffe so much at a loss. 'Sit here.' He caught Jude's shirt sleeve.

'My shoes——'

'Heavens, it's only a bit of water!' babbled Corey. 'You should see what gets on to this carpet sometimes. Don't worry.'

Somehow she must keep him here and get rid of

Tom. Jude seemed so ill at ease, so nervy. Maybe, she
thought, as she poured the tea, maybe he hadn't come
for her after all. Maybe it was something to do with the
cottage. Rent, possibly eviction at last, she thought
hysterically, her hand shaking.

'Sorry, I've slopped it,' she mumbled, her spirits
rapidly falling. Jude was rubbing his lip. He always
did that when he was about to take an unpleasant
decision or a difficult course of action. Oh, Jude! she
cried inside herself. Your son lies asleep upstairs!

Unable to sit near the two men, she wandered
around, tidying the debris of the day, moving around
the room swiftly and efficiently, watched happily by
Tom and morosely by Jude.

'Excuse me doing this,' she said, 'but if I don't keep
on top of it, it gets out of hand so quickly. And I have
to keep going because once I sit down I never get up.'

'Please don't let me stop you. I can see how busy you
are,' said Jude.

'Corey's just had an exhibition in Paris,' remarked
Tom.

'Congratulations,' said Jude politely.

'Thank you' She finished filling a box with the
bricks and curled up on the sofa. Tom handed her the
last slice of toast and she smiled absently at him. Jude
winced. 'You find time to work?' he asked, trying to
remain normal.

'Not much. While I was carrying Kal I built up a
huge stock of pieces. I still do some when he's asleep.
He's very good and sleeps a lot.'

'That's nice.'

'This is a picture of him,' said Corey, unable to
resist showing Jude his son. She fiddled with the clasp
of the huge silver locket around her neck and passed it
to Jude. No expression passed over his remote eyes

and Corey was bitterly disappointed, expecting some kind of recognition, or admiration at least.

'Nice child.' He handed back the warm locket hastily.

'Nice?' accused Tom. 'He's terrific! He . . .'

'Are you here for long?' asked Corey. It seemed unbelievably incongruous to have Tom singing the praises of Jude's son, and she couldn't cope with the irony of the situation.

'Not now.'

'What?'

'I've decided it's a flying visit. I've only just landed. I—I had one or two things to settle over here.'

'Well, let's hope you don't take back an English cold,' observed Tom.

'I didn't think of the rain. I arrived at the Manor and was surprised to see such a blaze of colour. I didn't expect the gardens to be kept up. When I saw them, I continued driving and came round to . . . to say thank you,' Jude finished lamely.

'I enjoyed working on them,' said Corey shortly.

'I'd forgotten how lovely the English countryside can be,' said Jude wistfully. 'You had no obligation to do anything, now the house is shut up.'

'No, but I couldn't let the gardens run to rack and ruin again. And your company is paying me a retainer,' she added.

'So you're back to Florida soon?' asked Tom.

Jude tapped his lip and lowered his eyes. 'Yes.'

'Where will you stay while you're here?' asked Corey, concerned that he might roam around looking for accommodation. He was in no fit state to do so in this weather.

'I cabled Mrs Morris. She's coming down on the evening train. She'll look after me till I leave.'

There was a lull. They were all behaving like polite strangers.

'Turin's going well,' said Tom brightly.

'Good.'

Tom tried again. 'Cottage looks nice, doesn't it?'

'Oh, yes,' interrupted Corey, remembering her manners. 'Thank you for designing such a *sympathetic* house for me. Radcliffe's in London told me it was your design. That was very kind. You must have been so busy. To be honest, all I expected was four walls and a roof with a door and a couple of windows.'

'You couldn't live in a nasty modern box,' said Jude shortly.

'I could if I had to, but I'm delighted that I don't. Forgetting the chaos inside, what do you think of your house?'

'My . . .' He rubbed his lip, pressing his elbow into his chest to contain the pain. His house? It belonged to Mr and Mrs Tom Gowrie-Dyson. And family. He must go. His eyes met Corey's. Tom had tamed her, gentled her. If only . . .

He raised his head. 'Listen!' he exclaimed, making them all jump.

Corey cocked her head to one side, trying to tune in to the possibility of Kal's cry.

Jude swore. 'It's a nightingale,' he said, the back of his neck chilling at the clear sound ringing out from the garden.

'Oh, that,' said Corey relieved. 'The nightingales have all gone, Jude. Flown away.'

'They would,' he muttered.

'Mmm. They're not daft enough to stay in England after the summer. That's a robin you can hear. Same family.'

'I thought it was a nightingale.' His face was stony,

his jaw clenched. Corey laughed nervously. Might he be close to a breakdown? He appeared to be so crushed by life.

A wail came from upstairs. 'Now *that* sound I recognise,' smiled Tom.

'Oh lor', he reckons he's missing something,' said Corey.

'Shall I go?' offered Tom eagerly.

She smiled in relief. Thank heavens for Kal. She'd have Jude to herself for a moment. 'You angel. Yes, please. My feet are just about to drop off. He's teething, you see,' she said to Jude, who stared resolutely ahead, not meeting her eyes. If only he would show interest! 'I've spent all day entertaining him and I'm longing for him to sleep.'

'I'll do my stock lullaby,' said Tom. ' "Ten Ton Tessie's the Girl for Me." '

Corey laughed. 'Idiot. You'll do 'Swing Low, Sweet Chariot' and like it.'

'O.K.' said Tom good-naturedly.

She watched as he mounted the stairs.

'More tea?' she murmured to Jude.

'No, thanks. I'll be off.' He attempted a polite thank you smile, but it died on his lips.

'If Mrs Morris isn't coming for an hour or so, maybe you'd better have scrambled egg supper with us,' said Corey. 'You're very welcome.'

'You've changed,' he said abruptly, not answering.

'Of course!' she replied, startled at his directness.

'You're ... happy.'

For a moment, she considered. It was a different happiness to the wild abandoned ecstasy she had experienced with Jude. There was no fulfilment of her own life as a woman, but then her son and her work took all her time, energy and love. Kal made her happy. Their gaze met, his almost pleading, hers confused.

The sound of Tom's creaking voice filtered down to them.

'Goodbye, Corey,' he rasped, snatching up his jacket.

'No, wait, *Jude*!'

Almost blindly he fled from the cottage and Corey ran to the window to see him running to his hire-car, trailing the jacket carelessly in the mud.

Within minutes, a bewildered Tom found himself leaving and Corey bolted the door behind him, clinging to its wooden panels, pressing her hands and cheek to the polished oak, the tears thickly falling.

Jude sat in the library, huddling over the gas fire. He'd changed into a thick sweater and casual trousers, but still felt chilled. The whole place offered no welcome. God, how he envied Tom, coming home from work to that haven, that roaring fire, that comfortable atmosphere, that beautiful child and glowing woman! He would have thought that a marriage with Tom was against all odds. A year ago he would have bet on its failure. But it seemed to be flourishing well enough.

Sighing, he poured himself another whisky. If he wasn't careful, he'd moon over that woman, building up their relationship out of all proportion. Restless, he meandered up to the bookshelves and ran his fingers along the spines, then stopped suddenly in his tracks and with his forefinger, traced the title which had caught his eye.

'*The Ursitory*. What the hell is that?' he muttered. It was a slim volume. As he idly flicked over the pages, one or two words stood out, seemingly in bold type. Gipsies—the book was about gipsies. Intrigued, he took it over to a chair and settled down.

'I'm in, Mr Radcliffe.' Mrs Morris's smiling face was peering around the door.

'I'm pleased to see you again,' he said, rising and welcoming her. 'You've no idea how much I've missed your cooking.'

'Hmm,' she said, a little sharply. 'That's just what I said to Miss Corey.'

She noted the small start that he made. 'Have you been to see her?' she asked, almost accusingly.

'Er—I popped in to thank her for making the gardens look so nice,' he said, immediately on the defensive.

It's not my place to interfere, sir——' she began.

'No, it's not.' Jude turned his back and took a gulp of whisky. 'Can you get me something to eat, Mrs Morris? Then I think I'll go straight to bed.'

'Very well, sir.' So, they were still sparring, were they? She'd soon sort them out!

Jude returned eagerly to the book. It was a fascinating story and he hardly looked up when his supper was brought in. Mrs Morris retired, sniffing.

So engrossed was he in the book that he had finished his meal before he realised. An hour later he had finished reading and was searching the shelves for other books—any books—about gipsies.

Late into the night he read, delving deep into the books which had been collected by Newton. He was beginning to understand Corey much better now. That strange mixture of abandon and wariness, the fear of 'capture', the underlying need to be part of a group which had been denied her.

Exhausted now, he was just about to leave the rest of the books for the next day, when he noticed one which was more used than the others. Its spine was broken and dirty and from the distortion of the covers, something had been stuffed into the pages. He lifted it out and it fell open immediately to reveal a folded piece of paper and a huge white feather.

When he opened the paper he recognised Newton's writing:.

'My dear Jude. If you have got this far then you are showing some real interest in Corey. Take care of her, because our society owes her some recompense for what we have done to her and her kin. Of all the people I know, you will understand her best because you have the same desire for freedom. That, of course, you get from your mother. We all fell in love with Catalina, but none of the Radcliffes were able to give her what she longed for.

'As far as Corey is concerned, you will know by now that she is a gipsy from the Kalderash tribe and therefore inherits a thousand years of skill in metalworking and other skills which I hope you will read about.

'Take her one day to the Camargue, where she can meet up with her people when they celebrate their Saint's Day. And one day, perhaps you will offer her this swan's feather as a token of your love. She will know what it means. Read this book and it will tell you. Remember, if you live your life with a tenth of the intensity that she does, you will be very happy.

'God bless you both, Newton.'

Pained by the irony of the situation, Jude leaned back in the chair and shut his eyes. Corey had settled with a man very similar to his father. Would she be faithless to him after a while? Maybe he didn't envy Tom now. He could be badly hurt.

The night was long and a sleepless one. Perversely, the next day was so brilliantly sunny that Jude had breakfast in the conservatory, relishing the late autumn warmth.

'Are you going out today, sir?' asked Mrs Morris, as she refilled the coffee pot.

'No, I'll sit and catch up on a bit of reading,' he said.

'Well, I was wondering . . . there's a lot to do here and if you've nothing special to do . . .'

'Of course I'll help. What do you want me to do?'

'I need some mushrooms for the stew.'

'Right, I'll go to the village.'

'Oh, no, Mr Radcliffe. They have those awful button mushrooms, grown indoors. If you go over Carson's field, there'll be some, and then Mr Carson has done a nice plump chicken for us.'

Going to Carson's farm would take him right past Corey's house. He couldn't resist going in, could he? She smiled in satisfaction at her scheming.

'I don't know the difference between mushrooms and poisonous toadstools,' protested Jude.

'That's all right, Mr Radcliffe, I know. You pick some for us and I'll make sure you're not poisoned. You'll like a nice tender chicken, won't you?'

He smiled at her. 'All right. But if I die I'll sue you. It's not a bad idea. A walk will blow away a few cobwebs.' He could do with some time to think, away from the distraction of the telephone. 'I'll just finish this book, then I'll go.'

Reaching for his coffee, he opened the broken book. The previous night he had read over half-way, fascinated and unwilling to put it down.

Relieved at the change in the weather, Corey hastily packed a simple lunch and prepared her son for a day out. Neither of them enjoyed staying indoors for long and his teething seemed to bother him less when he was happily occupied in the woods. For both their sakes, she must rebuild her life and stop dreaming about Jude. She strapped a rucksack on to her back and tucked him into the baby buggy, which was very battered from the frequent hauling over rough ground.

Outside, the air was clean and fresh after the rain. Champagne air.

'Mmmmm! Breathe that in, Jude,' she said. 'Hey, hear that?'

Obligingly, little Jude cocked his head, just like his mother, and pretended to be listening.

'That's a vixen's bark. We'll see if we can trace her lair. Right, we've got more than enough to keep us alive for a week. Let's go.'

Corey hadn't planned where they would go. Usually, on these jaunts, they followed their noses. Jude chortled happily as she sang one of her marching songs and she fancied that he was trying to join in.

Once through the wood, she decided to keep away from the Radcliffe meadow and make her way to Carson's land, the other side. As usual, she was combining a walk with filling her food store.

'Now,' she said, unstrapping Jude and setting him on the grass. Here, the soil was porous and the ground had already dried in the warm sunshine.

'Here's some Jack-go-to-bed-at-noon. Remember how to blow the seeds? See if you can tell me the time.'

His fat fist closed gently over the stem and he waved it around, watching the fine seeds drift away on the light breeze. Corey gathered a basketful of elderberries to make jam, keeping a careful eye on her son. He was engrossed in laboriously piling up bits of grass on to a dead leaf-beetle that he had found.

Further on, they stopped at the horse chestnut tree and Corey collected the chestnuts which had been driven down by the previous day's rain. Jude examined the shiny smooth chestnuts with interest and Corey told him all about playing conkers. The villagers smiled when they heard her talking to him as if he could understand. Corey knew he could and refused to use 'baby talk' with him. He was too serious—he'd think she was silly.

By now, weighed down with fruits of the autumn, Corey was ready to stop for lunch. She picked a spot on the edge of the wood and the meadow. As they ate, she wove a daisy chain for their heads, twining it with the lilac-blue Devil's Bit Scabious. Jude lifted a huge horse chestnut leaf and put it on his head too, laughing merrily, and she gathered him tightly to her, hugging him till he was breathless. He loved that. She rocked him on her lap, offering him the acorn 'hats' she had kept in case he was bored; his little fingers investigated every nook and cranny of them, smoothing around the little cup, totally absorbed.

She was so taken up with him that she did not hear the quiet footsteps approaching across the meadow. She began to croon a lullaby and gradually her son's thick black eyelashes dropped on to his cheeks, fluttering softly, then became still. He was breathtakingly beautiful. The lashes swept his flushed face, the black curls tumbled over his forehead and tipped his tiny ears. Corey traced each curl with her finger, kissing each one and kissing his button nose.

It was then that she heard a caught breath and turned to see Jude—Jude Radcliffe, a few yards away, hands stuffed in the pockets of his cotton jacket, turning from them.

'Don't go,' cried Corey. 'He's fast asleep, you won't disturb him. When he drops off nothing wakes him.'

Reluctantly Jude walked up and regarded her for a

moment before sitting down. Corey was stroking the smooth, bare little legs and feet of the child.

'I always seem to be intruding,' said Jude stiffly.

'No, you'll never be intruding.' She pressed a hand to her pounding heart. 'I see you've been on the forage, like us. What have you found?'

'Oh, I was under orders. A chicken from Carson's farm and mushrooms from the field. At least,' he added gloomily, 'I hope they're mushrooms.'

'Here, show me. I'll tell you. Yes, they're mushrooms. You won't be needing the last rites just yet.'

'You seem to have more of the countryside inside those baskets and on your heads than I can see around me,' he smiled. She looked quite lovely garlanded with the daisy chain. And the child.

'We've got chestnuts, acorns, elderberries, juniper berries and cobnuts,' she said, happy to have this stolen time with him. 'I like autumn time. Such a lot to do and find out and tell J—Kal.' Sometimes she found it difficult to remember that his name was secret to them both. She hoped he would understand as he grew older.

'He's very special to you, isn't he?'

'My treasure.'

'*Yours?*' Jude slanted his eyebrows at her.

'Well, he's on temporary loan, of course, till he's his own man.'

'Corey, I've found some books and papers of Newton's that I want you to have.'

She looked up in surprise.

'I've read the books. They're all about gipsies. Have you read them?'

'When I'd learnt to read Mr Wallace helped me to read through one—*In Sara's Tents*. I didn't know he had others. Why are you giving them to me? They're yours now.'

'Not really. You ought to have them. They're very interesting. Something else, Corey. My uncle left a sum of money to me, as you know. Part of that money is for you.'

Jude didn't mention that the money was to go to Corey if he didn't marry her. He couldn't bring himself to say that.

'Me? Why?'

'You know how fond Newton was of you. It's all in the papers. You can get a lawyer to O.K. it if you like, but I had to wait for a year and then . . . then I had to hand the money over to you. It should help a lot. Perhaps employ someone to look after—er—Kal when you want to work.'

'I look after him myself. No one else,' she said, her dark eyes on him. How thin he was! But thin or not, she was beginning again to feel the pull of his magnetism as they relaxed in the meadow. Her eyes kindled and he caught their fire.

God! She was sending messages to him even though Tom's child slept between them. Despite the situation, helplessly he leant towards her, answering the flare in her eyes with his own desire.

Unconsciously, Corey flung back her head like a nervous colt. As she did so, she arched the lines of her body and memories drove shafts of heat through him. She was fuller now and the free fall of her breasts under the loose shirt excited him beyond measure. Curse her!

Confident that her intuition was not playing her false, Corey fixed Jude with steady eyes and parted her lips in pleasure. He still wanted her! If only . . .

'Stay at the Manor,' she said huskily. 'I'd like you to

stay. It *must* be lived in. You *must* make that pond.'

'I can't, Corey. I daren't. Besides, I have my job to do.'

'You can design anywhere in the world. Even in rainy old England,' she coaxed.

It was tempting. Very tempting. But he couldn't cuckold a man on his own doorstep. How like his mother she was!

'Corey, I . . .'

To his concern, she edged closer to him and touched his face. 'Dear Jude,' she said, 'I can't believe you're shy. Neither can I believe you don't recognise this chemistry between us. You did before.'

'That was different.' He longed to catch her fingers and kiss each one. She seemed so tender.

'No difference at all. I still love you, Jude.'

'My God!' he gritted, glaring at her and the startled, waking child. 'I've told you before, you can't go around seducing every man you come across, gipsy or not. It's not decent!'

'And you never listened to my reply. I've only ever loved you.'

'Tom?' he queried, in a harsh voice.

'He's sweet. I feel nothing else.'

'Not even as Kal's father?'

Corey opened her eyes wide. So that was what he thought. Quite natural, she supposed. 'He's not Kal's father.'

The shock disturbed him deeply. 'Hmm. Typical of Tom to marry you to give the child a name.'

'Damn you, Jude!' She set aside her startled son, who was confused to hear his name spoken in anger. He crawled slowly away. 'I'd never marry a man for that. I have enough names for my son. Tom isn't my husband, he's only my friend.'

Jude frowned. 'Thank God for that. He's not right for you, Corey. Not even as an ex-lover.'

'You were my first and only lover,' she said in a low tone.

'But you didn't—you weren't . . .' He took a deep breath.

'Jude, I'd ridden horses for years. But I was a virgin when you made love to me, I swear on my son's head.'

'I came back to see you. Corey,' his voice lightened, 'I came back because——'

'*Jude!*' she exclaimed violently.

It was a moment before he realised she was shouting at the child—at Kal—who was just reaching for some black berries growing by the hedge. His little hand wavered and he turned to his mother, his lower lip trembling as she flung herself on him and dragged him away, tearing up the offending plant as she did so.

'Jude, my darling,' she said to her son, 'listen. These are bad. These are deadly nightshade. They will kill you. You mustn't ever touch berries like this.'

He reached out to a spray of elderberries, peeping from her basket.

'Oh, I know, that's what I pick. Were you trying to copy me and help? Poor darlin', what I shock I must have given you! Look, they're different. These are nasty, these are good. I'm sorry, my treasure. Shall we—oh!'

Standing sternly before her was Jude, his chest rising and falling, his eyes glowing smokily.

'*What* did you call him?' he whispered.

Her lips parted but no sound came from them. He crouched down on his haunches, very close.

'I said, what name did you give him?'

'Jude,' she breathed.

'He's called Kal.'

'Mmm. I made a mistake.'

He grasped her shoulders. 'I'll say you did!' Now what I want to know is, which is his real name? Tell me the truth, Corey, it's important.'

Miserably she lifted her chin, her own lip quivering.

'Gipsies have a secret name and a public name. I called him Kal after the Kalderash tribe. When we're on our own I call him Jude.'

'Why?'

She would have to tell him. The way he was looking, he wouldn't rest till he had prised it out of her.

'Because he was all I had of you when you left. Because he's your son.'

'*My* son?' He rose and walked away a few paces, full of anger. 'My child? And you weren't going to tell me?'

'What difference would it have made? Jude,' both of them looked at her. 'Jude—you won't take him from me, will you? Oh God! I couldn't bear it if you did! Please don't. I know you could give him a better life and I'm only a gipsy, but he loves me and I adore him. Please don't take him!'

She clasped her baby tightly to her breast and ran to Jude, her eyes filled with tears, unable to say any more because of the lump in her throat. She had never known such fear. Her lover had deserted her and now all her happiness was wrapped up in this child. Without him she'd be nothing.

To her surprise, Jude stretched out his hand and affectionately touched the daisy-chain circlet in her hair.

'I'm relieved to discover you can be still a bit silly,' he said softly. 'I thought you'd turned completely wise and womanly.'

'Silly?' she queried, wondering what was going on.

'Silly. Do you really think I'd take our son away from you after seeing how you love him and care for him?'

'Like teaching him to eat poisonous berries?' she said wryly, still shaking from the fright.

'I've never seen anyone so suited to be my son's— sorry,' he corrected, '*our* son's mother—than you. Put him down,' he ordered.

'He's still a bit upset,' she protested.

'Here.' Jude took his son from her arms and tucked his fat little legs around his neck. From his perch, little Jude gurgled with laughter, his impish face peering out at his mother through his father's thick brown hair. A surge of pleasure swept through Corey to see them together. She felt as if she had been reprieved from some awful sentence.

Holding carefully on to his son with one strong hand, trying to balance the joggling child, Jude reached inside the deep pockets of his cotton jacket. His fingers touched what he was searching for.

'Close your eyes,' he commanded sternly.

Frowning, she obeyed.

'Put out your hands.'

She felt something tickling, then it was as if there was nothing in her hands at all. He had been teasing her. She opened her eyes. Glancing down, she saw it. A swan's feather.

'Oh!' For the second time in a few minutes, her eyes filled with tears. He couldn't know what it meant. He had no idea how much his jokey present was hurting her.

Unable to keep his son in place much longer, Jude tucked him on to his hip and drew Corey to him.

'I've read all the books, Corey. This is a token. Do you know what it signifies?'

Wordlessly she nodded.

'For ever and ever I will defend you and protect you and love you like the swan cares for his mate. And that includes our child too. Corey, I tried living without you and it was hopeless. When I returned, I meant to beg your forgiveness and ask if you would give me a trial—throw me out if I tried to chain you too much. Seeing Tom with his socks on your mantelpiece was the most awful shock I've ever had. Apart, maybe, from seeing all those baby clothes around.'

'Oh, Jude,' she said, laying her head on his shoulder. 'I do love you. I'll keep the feather safely.'

'I want to marry you. But if you don't want that, please at least let me live with you. Anywhere, I don't care. As you said, I can design wherever I want. I'm handing over the major part of the management of Radcliffe's. I'd already arranged that, hoping that we'd get together. I knew I'd need time for you!'

'What will your parents say?' asked Corey.

'I'll tell you about them on the way back. Maybe that will help you to understand why I left you so cruelly.'

'You're back, that's all that matters,' she said, nuzzling into his chin.

'What about marriage?' he persisted. 'I think Jude here ought to have brothers and sisters.'

'Yes,' she answered, her eyes gleaming, 'so do I. Marriage would be wonderful.'

'You don't feel trapped, having said that?' Jude asked cautiously.

'No. My mother was right—freedom is within you. I feel totally fulfilled now. No one can take that from me.'

He gently stroked her face and tucked the black, errant wisps of hair behind her tiny ears.

'I'm going ask the best jeweller I know to design you a ring. I want her to make it like a swan's feather, curving around the finger, but not meeting. It mustn't meet. That means you're free in our marriage, Corey.'

As she clung tenderly to him, the desire rose between them both.

'No chance of this lad going to sleep again, is there?' he asked hopefully.

'No!' she laughed. 'Later,' came her promise. 'After bath-time.'

'Whose, his or ours?' he asked wickedly.

Her answering peal of laughter echoed around the wood and startled a flock of starlings who rose, chattering angrily.

Jude picked up the baskets and persuaded his son to travel in his buggy, bribed unashamedly with a lapful of Old-Man's-Beard which soon absorbed him.

Anyone looking across the meadow would have seen a family, tender and loving, walking slowly in the October sun, enjoying the sheer pleasure of being together in each other's company and relishing the promise of the years ahead.

Harlequin Presents

Coming Next Month

983 STANDING ON THE OUTSIDE Lindsay Armstrong
An Australian secretary is drawn out when her new boss goes out of his way to make her smile…enjoy life again. But what's the point if his heart still belongs to his childhood sweetheart?

984 DON'T ASK ME NOW Emma Darcy
How can a country girl from Armidale trust her heart to her uppercrust business partner? Especially when his attraction coincides with the renewed interest of the first man to reject her as not being good enough to marry.

985 ALL MY TOMORROWS Rosemary Hammond
In war-torn San Cristobal a nurse falls hard for an injured reporter, who then disappears from her life. She knows she must forget him. But how can she, when he finds her again in her home town.

986 FASCINATION Patricia Lake
Emotionally scarred by the last suitor shoved her way, a young American finds a merchant banker difficult to trust—particularly when their bedside wedding in her grandfather's hospital room is arranged by her grandfather and the groom!

987 LOVE IN THE DARK Charlotte Lamb
The barrister an Englishwoman once loved threatens to revive the scandal that drove them apart five years ago—unless she breaks off with her fiancé and marries him instead.

988 A GAME OF DECEIT Sandra Marton
A magazine reporter, traveling incognito, wangles an invitation to stay at a famous actor's private hideaway in the Mexican Sierra Madre. But she's the one who begins to feel vulnerable, afraid of being exposed.

989 VELVET PROMISE Carole Mortimer
A young divorcée returns to Jersey and falls in love with her ex-husband's cousin. But he still thinks she married for money. If only she could tell him how horribly wrong he is!

990 BITTERSWEET MARRIAGE Jeneth Murrey
Turndowns confuse a job-hunting woman until she discovers the souce of her bad luck—the powerful English businessman she once walked out on. Finally he's in a position to marry her!

Available in June wherever paperback books are sold, or through Harlequin Reader Service:

In the U.S.
901 Fuhrmann Blvd.
P.O. Box 1397
Buffalo, N.Y. 14240-1397

In Canada
P.O. Box 603
Fort Erie, Ontario
L2A 5X3

Take 4 books & a surprise gift FREE

SPECIAL LIMITED-TIME OFFER

Mail to   **Harlequin Reader Service®**

In the U.S.   In Canada
901 Fuhrmann Blvd.   P.O. Box 609
P.O. Box 1394   Fort Erie, Ontario
Buffalo, N.Y. 14240-1394   L2A 5X3

YES!   Please send me 4 free Harlequin Romance® novels and my free surprise gift. Then send me 6 brand-new novels every month as they come off the presses. Bill me at the low price of $1.66 each*—a 15% saving off the retail price. There are no shipping, handling or other hidden costs. There is no minimum number of books I must purchase. I can always return a shipment and cancel at any time. Even if I never buy another book from Harlequin, the 4 free novels and the surprise gift are mine to keep forever.   116 BPR BP7S

*$1.75 in Canada plus 69¢ postage and handling per shipment.

Name	(PLEASE PRINT)
Address	Apt. No.
City	State/Prov. Zip/Postal Code

This offer is limited to one order per household and not valid to present subscribers. Price is subject to change.   DOR-SUB-1A

ATTRACTIVE, SPACE SAVING BOOK RACK

Display your most prized novels on this handsome and sturdy book rack. The hand-rubbed walnut finish will blend into your library decor with quiet elegance, providing a practical organizer for your favorite hard-or soft-covered books.

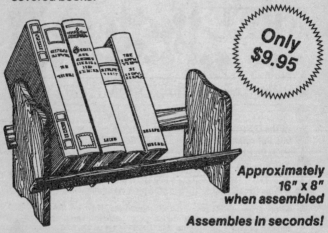

Only $9.95

Approximately 16" x 8" when assembled

Assembles in seconds!

To order, rush your name, address and zip code, along with a check or money order for $10.70* ($9.95 plus 75¢ postage and handling) payable to *Harlequin Reader Service*:

Harlequin Reader Service
Book Rack Offer
901 Fuhrmann Blvd.
P.O. Box 1325
Buffalo, NY 14269-1325

Offer not available in Canada.

BKR-1R

*New York residents add appropriate sales tax.

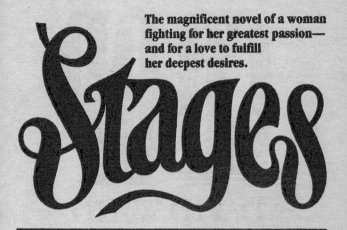
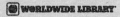

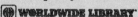